ALOHA CROSSING

Aloha Crossing

Pamela Bauer Mueller

Foreword by Michael Hingson

PIÑATA PUBLISHING
Jekyll Island, Georgia

Piñata Publishing
626 Old Plantation Road
Jekyll Island, GA 31527
912-635-9402

www.pinatapub.com

LIBRARY AND ARCHIVES CANADA CATALOGUING IN PUBLICATION

Bauer Mueller, Pamela

    Aloha crossing / Pamela Bauer Mueller.

Includes bibliographical references.

ISBN 978-0-9685097-9-1

    1. Title.

PS3552.A8365A64 2008   813'.54   C2007-907676-9

Cover art by Ian Kaszans
Typeset by Vancouver Desktop Publishing Centre
Printed and bound in China by Ray Hignell Services Inc.

I wish to dedicate this book to *Lions Club International*, "Knights of the Blind": the largest service organization in the world, with 1.3 million men and women in 200 countries and territories working together to answer the needs that challenge communities around the globe. My husband Michael and I are honored to be members of this awcsome organization.

Acknowledgments

Writing a book is never a solo endeavor. I relied heavily on my community of friends, family and colleagues for their various contributions.

To my **book publishing team,** endless thanks to each one of you! For most of you, this is our seventh team collaboration.

Patty Osborne, my typesetter, who magically turns each manuscript into a beautiful book.

Ray Hignell, my printer, thank you for your vision and enormous competence.

Pam Pollack, my editor, whose brilliant guidance and wise editing always make the end product much better.

Trip Giudici, editor, friend and fellow author, many thanks for your endless patience and outstanding work.

Sharon Castlen, my marketer (Integrated Marketing) and friend, thank you for your insights, encouragement and taking the extra step to be there for me.

A special word of thanks to **Michael Hingson,** National Public Affairs Director for *Guide Dogs for the Blind,* for reading the manuscript for accuracy and writing the warm Foreword to this book. Thank you for everything you do for the guide dog program and for the blind.

Dr. Jon Traer, fellow author and friend, your medical expertise and advice on rattlesnake bites is deeply appreciated.

To my dear friend **Diane Knight**, thank you for your brilliant editing of the final manuscript.

Louise Hooper and **Kim Belt**, your friendship inspired the character "Kimberly Louise."

Mimi and **Dennis Mulligan**, I enjoyed making you principal characters in this story. Thank you for so many years of love and friendship!

To my younger daughter **Ticiana Gordillo** and her husband **Ted,** thank you for sharing Aloha with me and loving her as much as you do.

Cassandra Coveney, my talented older daughter, thank you for your invaluable offer to edit the story and for your precise and loving counsel.

My mother, **Phyllis Bauer**, who also read, edited and advised, thank you for everything you've always been to me. And to my father **Don**, (whose memory is a blessing), I am grateful that you always believed in my ability to write.

Lastly, to my beloved and infinitely patient husband **Michael,** thank you for more reasons than I could ever name.

The support of each one of you helped make the writing of this story possible.

Foreword

Aloha Crossing is a wonderful and insightful book that will teach the reader what it is like to be blind. I hope you take to heart the lessons and concepts that you will discover in its pages. In *Aloha Crossing*, Kimberly Louise learns in some very graphic and vivid ways about her own abilities and inner strengths. She learns that through the use of alternative techniques she can do most of the same things that she had done as a sighted person and that she does them having as much fun as they do. She comes to realize that her life is worth just as much now as before. She learns that others value her life and her love and that blindness is not a factor when people form relationships with her. In short, Kimberly Louise adjusts to blindness in a very positive and realistic way.

Kimberly Louise's adjustment to blindness is strengthened, promoted, and supported by the relationship and attachment she has formed with Aloha, her guide dog, who we met in the book, *Hello, Goodbye, I Love You*. Kimberly Louise discovers what we at Guide Dogs for the Blind call the "guide dog lifestyle," which is all about two creatures, person and dog, forming a close bond and team relationship and then going out and doing whatever they wish to do.

During my 58 years I have learned that the blessing of my

Michael Hingson with Roselle (left) and Meryl (right), his current partner.

attitudes and beliefs about blindness didn't come because I was effectively born blind, but because of the attitudes and beliefs instilled in me by my parents. Later, those attitudes and beliefs were strengthened through my association with other blind people through the National Federation of the Blind: www.nfb.org.

In 2002, I left a successful 27-year career in computer sales and sales management to join the staff of Guide Dogs for the Blind. Today I travel the world speaking to organizations about my experiences and discussing the concepts of teamwork and trust, change, and overcoming adversity. I also speak about the human-animal bond. The speaking fees I earn go directly to support the efforts of Guide Dogs for the Blind. Please visit our web site at www.guidedogs.com. To explore my speaking availability to your company or organization, please visit www.michaelhingson.com.

The most dramatic proof about my philosophy on blindness came on September 11, 2001, when my fifth guide dog Roselle and I escaped from the 78th floor of Tower One of the World Trade Center in New York City. No one could have prepared us for what happened on 9/11. We survived that day because of the teamwork we exhibited as a natural part of our everyday world. However, the preparation was in the daily work and travel with each of my guide dogs and in the understanding that I could live and compete in a world that often doesn't comprehend that a blind person can be a successful part of it.

I believe that *Aloha Crossing* will peak your curiosity to learn more about guide dogs. Enjoy this beloved story! I think you'll find it as riveting as I did right up to the last page. I can't wait for the sequel!

—*Michael Hingson*
National Public Affairs Director, Guide Dogs for the Blind

Prologue

Aloha was struggling to breathe. Sleet-like wind and rain slapped her face, stinging her eyes, forcing her to turn away from the wind. She fought to keep afloat—soaked, cold and pelted by wind-driven rain.

She battled the angry river to swim toward the house. But with each stroke the current carried her further away from Kimberly Louise. Captured by the current, she was dragged under again and again. She tried grabbing onto floating pieces of wood but couldn't get a grip.

An undertow—a sucking, sweeping backwash—took her further away from the shore. Up, then down, slammed with spray, ripped inward, then shoved out. She kicked hard. A strong tide tugged at her hindquarters. Branches and other obstacles loomed up in front of her and banged against her heaving sides and injured leg.

The wake tide caught her and sucked her under again, spinning her body around and around before she could fight clear of it. Her lungs were almost bursting. With her mouth and throat full of water, Aloha fought and splashed in a delirium of terror. The hurricane's roiling clouds seemed like an avalanche bearing down on her.

When she finally surfaced, sputtering and panting, she gasped for just enough breath to fill her lungs. Her groping forepaws felt the impact of a submerged rock, and with her last ounce of strength she crawled feebly onto a narrow sand spit, where she collapsed and lay shivering, panting, and struggling for breath.

Chapter One

Master, go on, and I will follow thee, to the
last gasp, with truth and loyalty.
—William Shakespeare

"**A**loha, forward," she commanded gently. Kimberly Louise heard the parallel traffic begin—her signal that the light had turned green.

They stepped down to cross the street. Suddenly, Kimberly Louise felt Aloha's head jerk back violently as she roughly pushed her ribs against Kimberly Louise's legs. With the weight of her body, Aloha shoved her partner to the left. Jolted and unbalanced, Kimberly Louise fell backwards.

Someone was laying on the horn. HOOOOOONK!

She heard the screech of skidding tires and felt the rush of air as a car passed too closely.

SCREEEECH! THUD! Noises of a crash sounded in the distance. The world went gray.

Several cars slowed down to a stop. One woman hurried

over to the smashed car while her passenger ran to the woman lying on the ground.

"Call 911!" he shouted.

A pedestrian closed up her cell phone and called out, "They're already on their way!"

The driver saw a yellow Lab crouching by the woman, whimpering softly and licking her face. The dog glanced up as the man approached but didn't move away from her partner's side.

"Good dog," encouraged the man. "I'll just put my jacket on her to keep her warm." Moving slowly, he laid it over her and noted that her breathing was calm and even.

With sirens screaming, the police and ambulance arrived on the scene.

"Please stand back," a police officer commanded, skillfully directing the onlookers. "The medics are right behind us."

Aloha stayed resolutely beside Kimberly Louise while the paramedics examined her. When Aloha heard her moan, she nudged her companion with her moist nose.

Kimberly Louise slowly regained consciousness, feeling sore and dizzy. She blinked and focused on a face too close to her own.

"Can you hear me, Ma'am?" asked a faraway voice. Kimberly Louise was aware of the taste of vomit in her mouth. Hands were lifting her into an ambulance.

"Where's Aloha?" she asked, her heart dropping to her stomach. "Is she hurt?"

The police officer peered into her face. "She's right here next to me. She wouldn't leave your side. I've looked her over and she's fine," he answered with a reassuring smile.

At the sound of Kimberly Louise's voice, Aloha bounded into the ambulance and sat down as close to her partner as she could, licking her arms and face. Her tail thumped against the floor.

"That was a close one, Ma'am. A witness told me if your dog hadn't jerked you back, you would've been hit instead of just nicked."

A young man driving too fast had tried to beat the red light by turning quickly onto the street. Suddenly aware of a dog and woman crossing, he had slammed on the brakes and veered to the left, hitting a light post and grazing the woman's backside as she fell.

"Is the driver okay?" she asked, concern clouding her face.

"His injuries seem minimal, but he's been taken to the hospital for observation. We can tell you more after you've both been examined there," the paramedic told her, leaning over her stretcher. "Who do you want us to call?"

Kimberly Louise gave him the phone numbers for Mimi and David. "One of them will come for us," she said, rubbing Aloha's ears.

"That dog probably saved your life," he smiled, captivated by Aloha's maternal instinct toward her partner.

"Aloha's my angel from God," nodded Kimberly Louise. "I didn't tell her a thing back there when she jerked me out of harm's way. She just did what she needed to do."

"Amazing work," he said admiringly. "Miss Walker, have you been blind all your life?"

"No, just for a little over two years now. I was in a car accident on Jekyll Island." She paused, gripping Aloha's paw in her hand. "I was one of the lucky ones."

"So you've only had Aloha for . . .?"

"Less than a year," she answered. "And she's already given me an independence I thought I'd never have again."

When they reached the hospital, David and Mimi jumped up from their chairs in the emergency entrance.

"What happened, Kimberly Louise?" asked Mimi, her voice full of alarm. "David and I have been so worried! Are you okay?"

"Aloha saved my life, Mimi!" she said. Turning to smile at David, who had protectively reached for her hand, she was surprised to feel her cheek wet with tears.

Kimberly Louise was released after her examination and sent home with pain-killers and aspirin. Aside from minor scratches and bruises, she had survived the accident intact. The young driver had dislocated his shoulder and was still undergoing tests.

As Kimberly Louise lowered herself into the car, a worried expression crossed over her face.

"Do y'all think Aloha will still want to guide me after what happened to us today?"

David caught the dejection on her face. He and Mimi exchanged anxious glances.

"What do you think, Kimberly Louise? You know her best," David answered mildly.

A smile broke through. "She takes pride in guiding me. She knows she's my teammate, and I know she'll be there for me," she said convincingly. "Won't you, girl?"

Aloha gazed lovingly up at Kimberly Louise, stretching her neck to reach her fingertips with her black nose.

Chapter Two

A wise man is he who does not grieve for the things which he has not, but rejoices for those which he has.

—Epictetus, Greek philosopher

It seemed to Kimberly Louise that more than two years had gone by since she'd lost her sight. She only had to close her eyes to visualize memories in full detailed color. Reality hit when she opened them and could only see black shapes on a white background.

Her life had changed radically after the car accident on the Jekyll Island Causeway. She and her close friends David Wells and Mimi Ryan had been driving to Jekyll Island to play bridge with a small group. David had pulled over to the side of Highway 17 to wait out a rainstorm; then continued driving cautiously over the Causeway. Unexpectedly, a black Jeep appeared out of nowhere, spun out of control and slammed into them.

The results were devastating. Mimi and David sustained

only minor injuries, but one occupant in the Jeep was killed. Kimberly Louise lost her sight permanently.

During the long period of grief and denial that followed, her frustrations and intense anger clouded her thinking. She wallowed in self-pity for weeks at a time, refusing the comfort her family and friends offered. She explained that her sudden blindness felt like falling from a hilltop onto jagged rocks below.

"I've gone from summits of triumph to valleys of failure. Life has suddenly become a tortuous ride, and no one knows the outcome. I hate being so dependent on everyone. It's humiliating to have to ask you for help in everything I do."

Finally, Kimberly Louise understood that she had to accept her fate. She had always challenged herself, but her blindness was her greatest hurdle and required extraordinary courage. Reaching deeply for inner strength, she was now learning how to beat the odds.

"I'm slowly crossing the bridge from self-pity to hope," she told her grown children, John Henry and Julia, once she decided to attend the Roosevelt Warm Springs Institute for Rehabilitation. "When I return, I'll be walking with a cane and heading toward independence."

She finished the rehabilitation course and returned home a different woman. Several months later, Kimberly Louise made another life-changing decision: she applied for a guide dog. One of her instructors in Warm Springs convinced her that a guide dog would give her a different kind of freedom and offer companionship as well. When Guide Dogs for the Blind in California accepted her application and assigned her to a class on its Oregon campus, she knew she had made the right choice. She was ready to open her heart to a guide dog whom she felt would change her life and help her travel roads she thought she would never explore again.

And then she met Aloha, the dog chosen for her. Aloha was a medium-sized yellow Lab with a dark mark over her nose that she often wrinkled into an uncanny smile. By the time they met, Aloha had already completed six months of formal guide dog training, which consisted of leading a person from point to point in a straight line, stopping for curbs and stairs, and avoiding obstacles in her path. All of these activities involved obeying the trainer's commands through harness and voice communication.

Kimberly Louise arrived at the Oregon campus and had a few days to meet the other blind students and learn the routine of their daily activities. She and her roommate Barbie would receive their dogs on the same day, so they worked together to prepare their small room for two large dogs.

"Let's stand our suitcases one on top of the other in the closet," suggested Barbie. "Then we can get both kennels by our beds."

"Great idea! And we can move the chair to the corner,

since we only use it when someone visits," offered Kimberly Louise.

Kimberly Louise and Aloha bonded immediately. On their third week together, Kimberly Louise felt a spark of love pierce her heart. While walking with their trainer Rebecca through a suburban neighborhood, she pointed out that Aloha had completely ignored a teasing cat. Now Kimberly Louise understood that her canine partner concentrated only on *her* safety, and was there for *her* alone.

That afternoon she knelt by her bed and prayed for the first time since the car accident, thanking God for giving her back her freedom.

Then she phoned the boy who had given Aloha her "roots" and had prepared her for a life with a blind partner. She would finally meet Diego Escobár, Aloha's puppy raiser.

Chapter Three

I can do anything through Him who gives me strength.
—Philippians 4:13

Diego Escobár was just twelve years old when he became Aloha's puppy raiser. He and his best friend Jeremy Hunter had raised Aloha and her sister Alma from the time they were six weeks old, teaching them obedience and socialization. They worked and lived with the puppies for almost a year and a half, knowing that the dogs were only "on loan" to them. After the pups completed their basic training with their puppy raisers, they would be returned to the campus of Guide Dogs for the Blind for six to eight months of formal training.

Being a puppy raiser was a great job for Diego. An intelligent and reliable young man, he thrived on the responsibility of his position. Working with Aloha also helped him tone down his natural impatience and quick temper.

During their last weeks of formal training, the dogs were matched with blind partners waiting for their own guide dog. Every student was interviewed to ensure the best possible pairings. During the final four weeks, the human partner came to live at the school and work with his or her canine partner, under the watchful eye of the trainers. Finally, just before the graduation ceremony, each recipient was encouraged to meet his or her dog's puppy raiser.

So Kimberly Louise phoned Diego and invited him to dinner. Although they talked a little about themselves and shared some Aloha stories, Diego ended their time together bombarding Kimberly Louise with questions about the dog he hadn't seen for more than six months.

"Do you think she'll remember me, Miss Kimberly Louise?"

"Oh yes, Diego. I've learned that dogs never forget anyone they've known, and she lived with you for a year and a half! You will be amazed at how well she remembers you."

Then Kimberly Louise asked him how he felt about spending an hour with Aloha just before going on stage and turning Aloha's leash over to her.

"I think it will be tough," he replied honestly. "But I've already said goodbye to her once. Right now I'm just real excited to get to spend one more hour with her tomorrow."

Later, Diego told her that his time with Aloha was everything he expected and more. She not only remembered him, but also convinced him that he was still important in her life.

Relaxing on her wraparound porch in her favorite chair, Kimberly Louise faced the Hampton River and beyond to another coastal island, Little St. Simons Island, mentally recalling the lovely views. Surrounded by the beauty and tranquility of her southern home, her heart ached with pleasure as she recalled Diego's words on the podium the day of her graduation.

"Aloha is now where she was always meant to be. My family and I have raised her to be a hero for Miss Kimberly Louise. All through the training, they told us that raising the puppies is a gift of service to others. But I think it's also a gift of love to ourselves, because we'll have a part of our puppies in our hearts forever."

There wasn't a dry eye in the room that afternoon. Kimberly Louise's son John Henry had flown in from Atlanta to attend her graduation. Afterward, they joined Diego's family for refreshments, and during their conversation Kimberly Louise invited Diego and his family to visit her in Georgia. They accepted happily, promising to phone and email after Kimberly Louise returned home.

Kimberly Louise felt a quick burn of joy as she remembered another special moment. Diego took her aside and said, "Miss Kimberly Louise, do you know what *Aloha* means in Hawaiian?"

"I think it means *hello*, " she answered.

"Yes, but it means so much more," he said with a grin. "It means *hello*, *goodbye*, and *I love you*. Isn't that just perfect for her?"

And Aloha, hearing her name, had wrinkled her nose into her silly smile, thumped her tail and rolled onto her back, ready for a tummy rub.

Chapter Four

Yesterday is history. Tomorrow is a mystery. And today?
Today is a gift. That's why we call it the present.

—Babatunde Olatunji

The day after her graduation Kimberly Louise left the trains of northern Oregon and returned to her home on hot humid St. Simons Island, a small barrier island in southeastern Georgia.

As the plane began its descent into Brunswick, she felt a moment of panic and was overcome by a wave of sadness. She grieved that she was unable to see the forests of live oak trees draped with Spanish moss and the cypress and cedars lining the shore. Her memories overwhelmed her when she pictured the ocean's quivering foam and the gulls fluttering and splashing at the water's edge, as the glare of the sun cast a brilliant reflection streaming across the ocean at them.

She shook her head, exhaling deeply, and reached down to stroke Aloha's head.

"What's wrong with me?" she murmured to her partner.

"I'm having a pity party and forgetting that if I could see all of that, I wouldn't have you."

Aloha turned her face upward and sighed, as if she understood every word.

Kimberly Louise and Aloha made an imposing sight in the Brunswick Airport as they deplaned: a tall, straight-backed auburn-haired woman with startling blue eyes expertly led down the narrow steps by a harnessed yellow Labrador Retriever.

"Mama, we're over here!" called out Julia. Aloha pricked up her ears and waited for her command.

"Aloha, forward right," directed her partner with a soft voice. "Good girl."

Kimberly Louise broke into a huge grin when she heard the excited voices of her grandchildren, Tyler and Jonathan, running up to meet her.

"Hello, my sweeties," she cooed, greeting them with hugs and kisses.

Seven-year-old Tyler asked if she could pet Aloha, who was sitting quietly by Kimberly Louise's side and taking it all in.

"Of course you may, but move toward her slowly," suggested Kimberly Louise. "You too, Jonathan. Soon she'll know y'all are part of the family."

Her grown children lived in Atlanta. Since the accident they had made it a point to visit her frequently. Kimberly Louise was surprised to realize how quickly her grandson

Jonathan was growing up. Now nine years of age, his voice sounded lower than she remembered. She reached up to touch the top of his head.

"Jonathan, you've grown even taller. Are you still skinny?" she asked, giggling.

"Yes, Nana," he answered, reaching for her fingers and running them over his face, "and handsome too. Right Mama?"

"And modest as well," countered his mother with a smile.

"Jonathan, you know Aloha's puppy raiser Diego just turned thirteen. You would like him," said Kimberly Louise. "In fact, I'm going to invite him and his family out here for a visit. Who knows? Maybe you'll decide to be a puppy raiser when you're twelve."

"Me, too, Nana," interrupted Tyler. "I want my very own Aloha!"

Her grandchildren delighted in the sweet obedient dog, and wouldn't leave her side as they made their way out of the airport.

Julia drove them to her mother's house on Hampton Drive at the north end of St. Simons Island. As they pulled into the driveway, they were greeted with shouts of *Surprise!* Her closest friends had planned an unexpected homecoming dinner for her.

The evening had been wonderful and ended early. Around eight o'clock, Mimi drew her aside.

"We have so much to catch up on," she told her. "I can't

wait to walk the beach with you and Aloha and just talk and talk. I'll phone you tomorrow."

Kimberly Louise's friends knew she needed to rest and promised to phone her during the week. Julia accompanied her mother to her bedroom, now strangely unfamiliar, and stayed with her while she prepared for bed. Aloha never let her out of her sight.

With a mischievous grin, Kimberly Louise called Aloha up on the bed.

"We weren't supposed to do this at school," she explained to her daughter, "but now that she's home and there are no prying eyes, I'll let Aloha decide where she wants to sleep. Do you think she'll choose curling up on the bed with me, or laying down on the floor beside me?" Kimberly Louise giggled at the concept.

Julia laughed, relieved to see her mother adjusting so smoothly to her new life.

That homecoming to St. Simons Island with Aloha had taken place a year ago. The memories were tripping over her mind, charging at her from every angle. So much had happened since then: mostly good, positive and enriching experiences.

Kimberly Louise leaned back, lifting her fingers to her hair and loosening it from the tortoise shell clip. Sweet spring breezes warmed her face and called out to her to join them. She decided to take a walk.

"Aloha, come on girl. Let's walk to the marina." Aloha jumped up in anticipation.

During her walk, Kimberly Louise made up her mind that she would email Diego, inviting him and his family to visit them that summer.

Chapter Five

The way to see by Faith is to shut the eye of Reason.

—Benjamin Franklin

"Yes, Miss Kimberly Louise, those dates are great!" exclaimed Diego, enthusiastic about the plans she had made for his visit to Georgia.

"Are you sure your parents and Clara can't come too?" asked Kimberly Louise. "I have plenty of room. My grandchildren would love having all of you here in August. They're even planning their visit to overlap a week with yours."

"That's so cool! I wish my family could come but they want me to take a break from my summer job, and somebody's got to stay here to do my chores," he laughed. Diego was sorry his family couldn't join him, but knew that by coming alone he would have Aloha all to himself and spend time alone with her.

"Hey, I'm writing a term paper on hurricanes, and I read that Georgia and Florida have lots of them. Especially during the month I'll be visiting," he added.

"Well, yes and no. Florida certainly has had its share of hurricanes and so do North and South Carolina, but we haven't had one here in southeastern Georgia for well over a hundred years, so I wouldn't worry too much about it."

"I'm not *worried*, Miss Kimberly Louise. I think it would be a cool adventure!"

After they hung up, Kimberly Louise went online to buy the tickets for Diego. Using a screen reader—a small piece of software that converts what is on the screen into synthetic speech—she could surf the web by typing in commands on a keyboard, just like any sighted person would do, and hear the results with the screen reading software.

Diego was going to spend two weeks with her and Aloha; special time she knew he would cherish with the dog he raised. Lost in her thoughts, she didn't hear the knock on the door.

"Hey, is anybody home?" called out Mimi, walking in through the front door.

Kimberly Louise looked up in surprise. "Oh, hi Mimi. I'm just buying Diego's tickets for his visit in August." Mimi patted Aloha's head as she entered the room.

"Isn't it amazing what you can do with your computer

now? I remember when you thought you'd never learn Braille," Mimi said, her voice full of admiration.

"Me too, and then I thought I'd never be able to leave my cane behind and work with a guide dog. What little faith I had!" She turned toward her friend. "But you and David believed I could, and your support got me to where I am now."

Mimi reached over to hug her best friend.

"Hey, I came by to see if you want to go walking on the beach. We could stop at The King and Prince Hotel for lunch on the patio. What do you say?"

"I'm up for that! Just let me change my shoes and put on my blue sweater."

A slow smile spread over Mimi's face as she remembered Kimberly Louise's color marking system. After rehabilitation training at Warm Springs, her friends asked her how she recognized colors. She explained that she used small safety pins, one inside her white clothing, and two inside colored articles. She arranged the tiny pins in such a way as to identify colors: tilted slightly to the right for red, left for green, etc. She also had sewn Braille clothing tags into some of her clothing.

"And I pin my socks together in pairs so I won't wear one white and one dark one together," she added, giggling at their amazement.

She returned with her backpack and tennis shoes.

"Okay, now I'm ready. Let's go!"

When Aloha heard the familiar words *let's go*, she hurried across the room to stand beside the harness, tail wagging happily. Kimberly Louise and Mimi laughed at her predictable reaction.

They walked over the white dunes near the receding high tide, savoring the soft sand between their toes. For the first part of the walk Aloha was in harness, but after a while Mimi asked if she could throw her a Frisbee, so Kimberly Louise took Aloha off harness and let her run and fetch.

Aloha bounded joyfully through the small waves, always staying just a few feet away from her partner. Mimi threw the Frisbee for Aloha to retrieve again and again, until she was worn out. She had returned to Kimberly Louise's side by the time they reached the restaurant at the edge of the beach.

"Now I'm famished," stated Kimberly Louise. "Let's order! Aloha, here's some fresh water for you," she said, pulling the dish from her backpack.

After eating a large lunch they ordered ice cream and coffee.

"May I ask you something very personal, Kimberly Louise?" asked Mimi, adding milk to her steaming coffee.

"Sure. What is it?"

"Do you love David? I mean, as more than a friend."

Kimberly Louise slowly leaned back in her chair, pushing her hair away from her face.

"I'm not sure. I don't really know. After Larry died, I never really had a close male friend, and certainly not a boyfriend. But David is kind and treats me so well. It's just that I haven't thought about *loving* him."

"Hmm, well, he loves you. That's quite obvious."

"Mimi, has he told you that? He hasn't told me, and I would hope to be the first to know." Kimberly Louise was flushed and a little annoyed. "This feels so junior high to me!"

Mimi reached out and squeezed her hand. "No, Kimberly Louise, he hasn't told me. But if you could see the way he looks at you, you'd know. Would it make you happy if he told you he loved you?"

Unexpected goose bumps dotted her arms as Kimberly Louise closed her eyes.

"Oh Mimi, I don't know. I sort of feel frightened when I think about it. Maybe I need to just let my emotions flow freely as far as he's concerned." She smiled softly. "He's taking me to dinner tonight, so I'll try to just sit back and react spontaneously."

David had been a good friend for over six years. Since the accident, she was aware that he paid more attention to her than before, but Kimberly Louise didn't believe he was romantically interested in her. However, the thought didn't displease her. David was certainly a "catch" in the community. Yet Kimberly Louise had been too focused on her rehabilitation to allow her mind to accommodate her daydreams.

"Mimi, he hasn't put you up to this, has he?" she asked, eyes sparkling.

"No, girl, he hasn't. I just don't want you to miss out on a fabulous opportunity because you haven't got a clue, so I told you what I think. Now, the rest is up to you."

Giggling, they linked arms and began strolling back to East Beach. Aloha, now in her harness, kept pace at her partner's heels. She occasionally threw a glance over her shoulder, studying them. It was as though she trusted Mimi's guidance, yet knew that *she* was responsible for Kimberly Louise's safety. Aloha was her shepherd.

Chapter Six

There is no use trying, said Alice; one can't believe impossible things. I dare say you haven't had much practice, said the Queen. When I was your age, I always did it for half an hour a day. Why, sometimes I've believed as many as six impossible things before breakfast.

—Lewis Carroll

Sunshine beat down on the crushed oyster-shell drive, and a lazy early summer wind raised yellow dust that trailed in clouds down the street. The sun steamed the nearby marsh, giving off heat like a golden shower of light. David, Kimberly Louise and her grandchildren walked the oyster-shell roads as they explored Fort King George in the tiny coastal town of Darien.

"Did you know this fort was built before General Oglethorpe landed in Savannah in 1733?" David asked Kimberly Louise.

"No, I didn't. I only remember that he brought the Scottish Highlanders to live here later on," she said, calling Tyler and

Jonathan over to join them. "Come listen to what David is telling us about this fort's history."

"Well, it was named after King George I of England, who sent British settlers here to establish a town. A few years later Oglethorpe brought the Scottish Highlanders on his second journey to Savannah and they lived in nearby Darien. They were fierce fighters who also learned to cut and mill the local timber. Eventually, they built the town of Darien into a major seaport."

They reached the three-story cypress blockhouse.

"Aloha forward, inside," instructed Kimberly Louise.

Aloha guided her carefully up the stairs. Her space perception and the ease with which she led Kimberly Louise amazed people who watched her. Feeling subtle signals through the harness handle, Aloha seemed to respond intuitively to Kimberly Louise's intentions. They formed an incredible team.

A couple was watching them and complimented Aloha's behavior.

"She minds beautifully," the woman observed. "You must be so proud of her."

Kimberly Louise smiled her thanks.

"Hey, Nana, has Aloha ever messed up?" asked Jonathan.

"Let me think," she mused, her blue eyes as quick and friendly as her smile. "Oh yes, I can remember one time recently during our flight to Atlanta."

"Were you coming to see us?" Little Tyler knew the answer, but asked anyway.

"Yes, and I was napping in my seat. Aloha was stretched out at my feet, with her head under the seat of the passenger in front of me. I woke up to the sound of paper crumbling and smacking noises. Aloha had discovered a lunch bag under the seat of the person in front of me, nosed into it and was eagerly gobbling down her lunch."

"Aloha, you did *that*?" asked Jonathan, incredulously.

"Nana, did you spank her?" wondered Tyler.

"No, dear, I didn't. Once she realized I had caught her in the act, she was ashamed. And the lady in front of us was laughing so hard," remembered Kimberly Louise, her face breaking into a wide grin.

"I think that's probably the only thing Aloha's done that wasn't in her obedience training, isn't it dear?" asked David, placing his hand lightly on her shoulder.

"Well, she sleeps on my bed, but that's my fault. Do you remember I told you that she was trained to never jump up on any furniture? Well, that's certainly changed. And there may be a few other things that I'm too lax on, but they escape my mind at the moment," said Kimberly Louise. "Now let's go back outside to watch the reenactment of the Battle of the Bloody Marsh. I think Aloha is ready for her nap!"

"Nana, she won't be able to sleep with all that noise," argued Tyler.

"Oh no? Just watch her!" Kimberly Louise knew that once Aloha realized her partner was safe, she could sleep through anything.

After the reenactment, they joined other visitors for a typical Spanish dinner served buffet style on long tables. The sweet aroma of baked bread hung in the evening air as they dug into large plates of hot corn cakes, baked fish, barbequed venison, long grained rice, hominy grits, green vegetables, and warm dark bread, followed by a delicious custard dessert called flan.

Kimberly Louise sliced into her venison with a sharp knife, savoring the tangy flavor of the meat.

"Thanks, David, for preparing my plate," she smiled, brushing her fingers over his arm. "It's hard for me to appreciate that you serve me because you are a gentleman, and not because I'm blind."

David smiled and squeezed her hand.

"Mr. Wells, how do you know where to put Nana's food?" inquired Tyler, never missing a thing.

"Good question, Tyler," smiled David. "She taught me to place the meat at six o'clock, the rice at nine o'clock, the vegetables from two to four o'clock and the rest at twelve o'clock. Then she knows where everything is."

"And her drinks are always at twelve o'clock too," added Jonathan, noticing her iced tea and water glasses.

"Yes, but they're at the top of my plate, so even if they aren't exactly at twelve o'clock, I can still find them," chuckled Kimberly Louise, touching her lips with her linen napkin.

"And you learned all of that at Warm Springs, right Nana?" asked the inquisitive Tyler.

"Oh yes, sweetie, and a lot more. When I first started cutting my meat, they positioned my hands so I'd learn how to reverse the fork to the left hand and the knife in the right. That's why I'm so good at chopping and dicing with knives now."

"I want to go to that school one day," declared Tyler. "Just in case I go blind later."

"That's really dumb, Tyler. You only go *if* you are already blind, silly," countered Jonathan.

"And I also want a dog like Aloha to help me do everything," she continued, ignoring her brother. "Look at her. She's watching Nana with one eye open and sleeping with the other."

"Hey, look at the sun!" exclaimed David, pointing out the gold-washed sky as the sun was taking a final dunk into the horizon.

As they headed south back to St. Simons Island, they watched the shining reflection of sunlight dropping over the marshes of the Altamaha River, leaving a ruddy glow on the waters.

Chapter Seven

Come to me, all you who are weary and burdened,
and I will give you rest.

—Matthew 11:28

Aloha sensed that Kimberly Louise was in a terrible mood. She tried to follow her around the house, and that annoyed her mistress even more.

"Aloha, go lie down on the mat by your harness," she snapped.

Bowing her head Aloha obeyed, dark eyes filled with sorrow.

A small group of friends was going to Jacksonville to see a play that afternoon. At first, Kimberly Louise had agreed to join them, but then changed her mind. She was angry that she could no longer see the actors or sets, and couldn't enjoy the spectacular views of the St. Johns River from the Landing, where they would later sit and dine after the play.

"I'm fed up with being blind," she told Mimi over the phone. "I'd just be grumpy and ruin your day."

"Kimberly Louise, that's nonsense. Once we get going, we'll make you laugh, and you'll have a good time."

"No, I won't. I've spent the last few days coming to terms with how the rest of my life will be, and it's not pretty. Just go ahead without me, and hopefully I'll snap out of this funk soon."

She needed to finish preparations for the arrival of Diego and her grandchildren the following week. Walking quickly through the house in search of her yearly calendar, she scraped her thigh against the corner of the dining room table.

"OUCH! That hurts!" she cried out, tears smarting her eyes.

Aloha, watching her from the corner of the room with her tail carefully folded under her paws, twisted her head to one side and whined softly.

"It's okay, girlfriend. I'll be fine," she murmured to her partner.

After lunch, she and Aloha went into the sunroom to relax. Kimberly Louise was still out of sorts and decided not to read. Aloha, confused, placed a timid paw on Kimberly Louise's leg and stroked it lightly.

"Stop that, Aloha! Leave me alone. I don't feel like talking today. Sorry."

Aloha rested her chin on her partner's knee and sat very still, waiting patiently.

The doorbell rang. With a loud groan, Kimberly Louise walked to the door.

"Hello, Kimberly Louise." David stood smiling at the entrance.

"Oh, I thought you were going to the play." Her voice was sharp and clipped.

"May I come in?" he asked her lightly.

"Of course." She stepped aside. "I'm sorry David. I'm in a snit today and forgot my manners."

David walked to the sunroom and greeted Aloha, still waiting patiently for her next command.

"I decided not to go with the others. I prefer visiting you," he said smoothly.

"Look David, this isn't a good time for a visit. I'm wallowing in self pity today and I won't be pleasant company." She hadn't meant for the words to come out like they did, so tough and harsh.

"Let's have a nice cup of tea and talk about it."

Kimberly Louise smiled. "Good idea, David. Let me brew us some tea," she suggested.

"I know where everything is, dear. Please let me do it today," offered David.

As David prepared the tea, Kimberly Louise lowered herself to the floor next to Aloha.

Rubbing Aloha's head, she whispered, "Good girl, Aloha.

Forgive me for my bad mood. Thanks for being so under-standing and loving me in spite of myself." She kissed Aloha's nose and felt tears brimming in her eyes. She fought to hold them back, and then gave up.

Aloha thumped her tail and nuzzled into her hand. A moment later she was licking the tears coursing down Kimberly Louise's face.

David quietly entered the room and found them huddled together on the floor. Setting down the tray, he knelt down beside them.

"Come here, my dear. Tell me what happened today," he coaxed, locking his arms around her shoulders.

"Oh, David, I'm such a mess. Everything seems so bleak and dark in my future," she sobbed. David watched the stub-bornness in her eyes slowly turning fragile.

"I hate being blind. I hate losing control of my life. Nobody can possibly understand what that's like." Tears spiked her eyelashes.

The three of them remained on the floor while Kimberly Louise poured out her heart. She was furious at the injustice of her freak accident, bemoaned her uncertain future, railed out against sighted people who could never understand the bleakness of her dark world, and wept angrily in his arms.

David kissed the crown of her head and gently tucked stray pieces of long wet curls behind her ears.

Looking into her swollen eyes, he smiled with under-standing.

"We will always be here with you to help you face that darkness, my love. Aloha and I will never leave you. Together, we can handle anything."

Kimberly Louise pulled in a short gasp of air and raised her head. "What do you mean?"

He lifted her face and stroked it tenderly; a gentle brush-ing of his fingers.

"That I want to be with you always and want to help you work through your frustrations. Don't you know how much I admire your strength and faith? You've come so far, Kimberly Louise. Don't give up now. Fight for your future!"

Aloha watched them nervously, turning her face from one to the other, puzzled but reassured by the soft tone of David's voice.

"Sweetheart, do you know how immense redwood trees can withstand high winds even though they have remarkably shallow roots?"

"No, how?" she said.

"They hold each other up. Few other trees interlock their roots with the tenacity of the redwood. Only when they stand together, allowing their roots to weave seamlessly into each other, are the redwoods truly strong."

Kimberly Louise raised herself to her knees, wiping her cheeks.

"Oh David, thank you. You always know how to find the beauty in life." She struggled with her next words, but finally added softly. "It seems that when I'm with you I can sit still and let contentment wash over me. Please don't give up on me."

He took her in his arms, holding her through the rest of her private storm. Then he kissed her, a long gentle kiss that sealed his love.

Chapter Eight

Many things I have tried to grasp and have lost.
That which I have placed in God's hands, I still have.

—Martin Luther

After David left, Kimberly Louise sat for a long while and thought about his words. For over two years she had been pressing so sharply against life that she was often hurt by it in return. She needed to find her way around loneliness and fear, and stop being a slave to her emotions.

"Just let go, dear one, and let contentment come to you," David told her as he kissed her again before walking down the front steps.

A few months after her car accident, she decided not to stay paralyzed in her pain and loss, but rather grow toward her healing. That decision had turned her fear into hope.

"Aloha, are you afraid of anything?" she asked her companion.

Aloha looked at her with a long, loving gaze.

"Well, can you believe that I was once afraid of dogs?"

Kimberly Louise smiled as she looked down at her partner, who had stretched out at her feet with one ear lifted toward the sound of her voice.

"Oh yes I was! As a young child, I distrusted them and wasn't very nice to them. My grandfather noticed it and helped me adjust my attitude," she giggled, treasuring the memory of her Grandpa and their close bond.

Aloha lazily lifted her head from her paws and studied Kimberly Louise with a long look.

"He told me a story about himself that changed my life forever. You see Aloha, he was also afraid of dogs for a long time, until he met one that taught him what they were really all about." She tucked her legs under her on the sofa and patted her knees—Aloha's cue to rest her chin there.

On hot summer afternoons Kimberly Louise and Aloha usually treated themselves to several lazy hours in the air-conditioned sunroom. After reading on her computer or enjoying a novel in Braille, Kimberly Louise often shared stories with Aloha. They looked forward to this afternoon ritual, sometimes napping together on the wicker sofa below the gently blowing fan.

"You know, my Grandpa worked in the Philippines in the early 1900's for about three years. When it was time to return home, he booked the very first ship out. Unfortunately, that ship happened to be a run-down excursion boat.

He soon regretted his hasty decision, especially when he discovered that a huge Great Dane would be sharing ship space with him.

"Now Grandpa had always disliked dogs simply because he was afraid of them. This huge animal realized that and kept its distance, spending time with the crew who appreciated its magnificence. Grandpa told me that the dog's tail seemed as big around as his arm, and its mouth the size of a crater.

"After a week at sea, the boat caught fire and burned quickly. All hands were struggling with the few safety boats onboard, but Grandpa remembered a life raft in the aft of the boat. While flames were eating up the deck, he managed to hack the life raft loose with his knife and threw a cask of water and some crackers he had brought up from the galley inside it.

"After a great struggle, he lifted one end of the heavy raft onto the rail and just as the water was reaching the edge of the deck, threw himself into the raft and pushed it over the side.

"Grandpa said he was thrashing under water for what seemed like an eternity and felt like his lungs would burst. Eventually the raft surfaced; he vaguely remembered laying there, his limbs spread across the bottom, half-conscious. When he finally came to, he spat out a mouthful of water and saw that the cask of water and crackers were still in the raft. But the sailcloth had vanished, and he felt desperate and afraid.

"The sea was fairly calm, and as he looked about, he saw no humans; only wreckage. He believed every man on board had gone down with the ship.

"Suddenly he spotted the huge head of the dog coming toward him through the water! That dog must have known that Grandpa's raft was the only thing afloat large enough to hold it. Grandpa was petrified, fearing the demon dog was coming to devour him. He told me his teeth rattled and he trembled all over.

"The dog reached the raft and lifted one large paw and then the other up onto the side. The top of the raft rose up six or eight inches above the water, and it took great effort as the dog tried to climb aboard. Grandpa wanted to kick it back into the water, but didn't dare. The dog struggled mightily, again and again rearing its enormous shoulders out of the water, only to slide helplessly back in each time the raft lurched.

"Finally a wave favored the beast and it was able to catch the edge of the under platform with one huge hind foot. Heaving its large bulk over the edge, the Great Dane lay sprawled at Grandpa's feet, trembling and exhausted."

Kimberly Louise held Aloha's head between her hands and stroked her ears. Aloha nuzzled into her hands. Telling the story had brought back the same strong emotional reaction as the time Grandpa had shared it with her. Aloha snuggled closer and smiled at her with gentle and wise eyes.

"Grandpa hated and feared that powerful dog. He cowered as the dog stood up, shook itself, and looked contemptuously at Grandpa. Slowly it lumbered to the other end of the raft and lay down, settling in.

"The sea was calm and they drifted slowly on the empty sea. At nightfall, Grandpa opened the box and ate some crackers, noticing how the dog watched him closely, but didn't beg. Then he drank some water, and refused to share that either.

"The gentle motion of the raft lulled them to sleep, even though Grandpa struggled to stay awake and keep an eye on the Great Dane. The few times he woke up, the dog was watching him too."

Kimberly Louise paused; Aloha was still watching her and following the story.

"The next morning, Grandpa opened the can of crackers again and ate a few. He began to fear the huge dog might eat him if it got too hungry, so he decided to share what he had. He tossed the dog a cracker. The dog didn't touch it; just lay there with its great head on its paws, staring at my grandfather. Obviously the dog distrusted Grandpa as much as Grandpa distrusted it.

"Finally the beast arose, sniffed suspiciously at the cracker and looked back at Grandpa.

"It's all right; eat it!" Grandpa ordered. Only then did the dog eat the cracker, looking up expectantly after the last swallow. Grandpa threw it a few more crackers; then told the dog they had to pace themselves. The dog lay down and licked its chops, perfectly understanding the situation.

Chapter Nine

Dogs live with man as courtiers round a monarch, steeped in the flattery of his notice and enriched with sinecures.

—Robert Louis Stevenson

"Late that afternoon a steamer came into view and Grandpa jumped up, waving and shouting while the dog watched with interest. Sadly, that ship turned and sailed away. Grandpa sighed and gave the dog food and water, and was rewarded by the wagging of the great tail. That night Grandpa spoke to the dog, surprising both of them.

"Lonesome out here, isn't it?" he said, and the beast answered with a deep sound in its throat—not a growl but an answer to the question.

"Then Grandpa began to talk about everything—his family, his friends, his prayers—and the dog listened. The huge animal slowly approached him and sank down at his feet, curling its body into a semicircle. Grandpa suddenly realized that the dog had dignity. It wanted to be friendly, but would not presume. Later they fell into a deep sleep.

"Grandpa was awakened by the pitching of the raft and the dog standing in the middle, looking at him in evident alarm. The blackness of the horizon meant a storm would hit them soon. Grandpa tied a rope around his waist and waited. When the storm struck, the raft pitched and tossed, almost engulfed by the waves. The dog skidded and slid on the wet deck, its hindquarters actually slipping over the edge. A wave swept over them, but the dog clung to the floor and held on. As the raft suddenly righted itself, Grandpa was stunned by the look on the dog's face—a look of fear, pleading, and silent courage. He realized that the dog knew that Grandpa was the master, and it was only a dog.

"Grandpa raised himself up, loosened the spare rope he had saved and tied it around the dog's body, clutching tightly with his hand. The beast's great weight almost pulled his arm from its socket, but Grandpa held on mightily. Just as quickly as it began, the storm passed. Both knew they were safe. That evening Grandpa named the dog Peter and they slept side by side.

On the fourth day, when the provisions were gone, Grandpa saw a steamer heading directly toward them. He began to shout and wave his faded blue navy coat.

"She's coming our way, Peter!" he cried, caressing the

dog's ears and head for the first time. As he patted the beast, Peter rapped furiously with his tail. Grandpa stroked its neck, back and flanks as the dog quivered with joy, leaning its huge body against him and nuzzling his arm with its black moist nose.

"Then Grandpa said the dog did something incredible, Aloha," murmured Kimberly Louise, with a catch in her throat. "Peter bowed his head and licked his shoe."

She paused a moment. "A feeling of shame and unworthiness came over my grandfather. He realized how completely he had misunderstood his new friend. Why would this powerful creature lick his shoe?"

Kimberly Louise reached for a tissue as Aloha gazed up at her with devotion. "All fear and distrust left my grandfather and a feeling of comradeship and understanding took their place. They had been through so much together, and that noble creature had licked his shoe! Grandpa turned to me and smiled softly, confessing that suddenly he realized he loved that dog. He threw his arms around Peter's neck and told him so.

"The steamer crawled along, showing no sign of observing them. Grandpa was beyond dismay. He could see the captain on the bridge, and other people below, but knew that they were so low in the water it was impossible to be seen. He turned to Peter.

"Speak, old man! Speak to them!" he pleaded as the dog closely watched Grandpa.

"Then a roar like that of ten lions rolled out over the blue Pacific. Again and again Peter called to them with his deep and powerful voice. His great sides heaved with the mighty effort, his cavernous mouth open, and his head raised high.

"Good job, old man!" Grandpa encouraged, as again and again that magnificent voice boomed forth.

"When my Grandpa saw figures peering out over the side of the ship, he shook his tattered coat in the whipping wind, dancing up and down in the lifeboat. Peter roared some more.

"After they were rescued, Grandpa slept twenty-four hours straight. When he woke up, Peter was sitting beside his bunk, and when he turned to look at him, the dog lifted one great paw and placed it gently on his arm."

Kimberly Louise paused for a long moment. "When he finished his story, I asked my grandfather if he took Peter home with him. He smiled and nodded, his tired eyes filling with tears. I asked him if he still had that dog, because I really wanted to meet him. Grandpa didn't answer and looked away, shaking his head sorrowfully. A look of great sadness washed over his face."

Kimberly Louise leaned forward to plant a huge kiss on Aloha's nose. "But you see, Dear One," she murmured, "because of Grandpa's amazing story, I lost my fear of dogs. And that must have been part of God's plan for me, because many years later He brought you into my life."

Chapter Ten

A bird doesn't sing because it has an answer;
it sings because it has a song.

—Maya Angelou

Diego was so excited he couldn't sit still as the plane descended into the Jacksonville, Florida airport. He kept thinking about the trip his family had taken to Florida two years ago, when they visited Disney World, Cocoa Beach and St. Augustine. Having Aloha with them had made it such a special trip. Now he was returning to the east coast and would be with Aloha once again!

How long had it been since he'd seen her? Was it just a year ago when he'd walked her up on the stage and turned her over to Kimberly Louise? That was the last time he'd been able to hug her. She had remembered him then after their first six-month separation when Aloha was undergoing formal harness training, but she'd met so many people since then. Would she remember him now? Other puppy raisers said she would, but Diego wasn't convinced.

He quickly spotted her in the baggage area, proud and beautiful, sitting next to Kimberly Louise. Two children were near them, probably her grandchildren, pushing around an empty baggage cart, aiming it at each other and then dodging it when it careened their way. A tall man was standing next to Kimberly Louise, holding her hand. Diego stared at Aloha, a knot rising in his throat.

Then she lifted up her nose and sniffed. Searching through the crowd, she found him. Up went her splendid head. She came to her feet with a shudder, and the message was transmitted through the harness.

"Diego?" Kimberly Louise called out softly. She turned to David. "Aloha knows he's here."

Diego greeted her as he approached. "Hi Miss Kimberly Louise. I'm over here," he answered, blown away at the sight of his beloved dog.

"Wait, Diego. Stop there. Let me take her off harness so she can greet you properly," she said, removing the harness. "Go on girl. Go see Diego."

Aloha stood perfectly still as she peered intently at Diego. Then she began to creep toward him, one slow step at a time, crouching low. Her eyes never left Diego's dazed face. Inch by inch she continued her dramatic crawling advances.

Diego finally found his voice. "Aloha, *ven acá, muchachita* (come here, little girl)," he encouraged, his throat closing up.

Aloha yelped, as though struck. She flew through the air, hurling herself on her long-lost puppy raiser, insane with joy. Diego thought the impact would knock him over, but then she stood on her back legs and lifted both front paws to his shoulder. After licking his face, she began whirling around him in galloping circles. Finally, she ended the performance by dropping to his feet, laying her head on his shoe and whimpering with happiness.

The incredulous grandchildren rushed over to Diego. "Wow!" said Jonathan. "I've never seen her do that!"

Kimberly Louise, leaning on David, reached Diego's side. She hugged him fiercely, hoping he wouldn't notice the tears slipping down her cheeks. She had heard Aloha's welcome, and was deeply moved by it.

"And you worried she might not remember you," she said quietly.

Diego, still awestruck, reached up to return her embrace. An endearing smile lighted his face.

"Hey, Miss Kimberly Louise. I'm so glad she still knows me," he said, choking on his words.

"*Knows you*, Diego? She *loves you*, silly boy. Just listen to her."

David held out his hand. "I'm David Wells, Diego. And these are Tyler and Jonathan. Welcome to the south."

Diego released Aloha to shake David's extended hand. Both grandchildren stood by quietly, still hypnotized by Aloha's effusive greeting.

"Aloha, let's put your harness back on now and go collect Diego's bags," suggested Kimberly Louise.

Still fiercely wagging her tail, Aloha returned to her partner's side. Tyler and Jonathan resumed their chattering, cross-examining Diego about his trip and his puppy raising days. Soon the bags were in the cart and they were headed for the parking garage.

"Diego, I have a feeling you'd like to ride in the back with Aloha," smiled Kimberly Louise. "It's an hour and a half trip, and you'd have a chance to make up for lost time."

"Me, too," cried out Tyler. "I want to sit back there with them!"

"Good," announced Jonathan. "I'll have the second seat all to myself and I can listen to my music," he added with a grin.

Releasing a long happy sigh, Diego leaned back into the seat, Aloha's head resting on his knee. He couldn't remember feeling such joy since the day he had first met her as a six-week old puppy.

"Good girl, *muchachita*. I know we're going to have another awesome vacation together!"

Chapter Eleven

God be praised; that to believing souls gives
light in darkness, comfort in despair.
    —William Shakespeare

"**H**ere we are!" David Wells told everyone as they pulled into the driveway. Diego stared at the stately three-story home, surrounded by a wraparound porch and bordered by a colorful English garden. He noticed the dark red tiled sloping roof and the elegant Mediterranean architecture.

"Miss Kimberly Louise, is *this* your house?"

"Yes, dear, and Aloha's too. And now it's yours and Tyler's and Jonathan's as well," she answered graciously.

"WOW! It's the nicest house I've ever seen!" he blurted out.

"And your room is really cool," added Tyler. "You're on the third floor, and me and Jonathan have rooms on the second floor, near Nana."

"Where does Aloha sleep?" asked Diego.

"On my bed," laughed Kimberly Louise. "I know you had to teach her to stay off furniture, but I let her sleep on my bed," she confessed.

"That's okay, Miss Kimberly Louise," laughed Diego. "It was always hard keeping her off the sofa at our house." He smiled at Aloha, who was tilting her head slowly from one to the other as they mentioned her name.

Mr. Wells carried Diego's suitcase up the front stairs. "Let's get you settled, and then we'll give you a tour of the neighborhood," he suggested.

Aloha, now off leash, followed them up the stairs and into Diego's room. As they passed the porch, Diego saw at least six rocking chairs.

"Rocking chairs!" he exclaimed. "That's what you always see in pictures of the south!"

"Well, you are in the south, silly," said Tyler. "I'll show you how to rock because it's one of my favorite things too."

The others laughed. Kimberly Louise suggested they all give Diego some time to unpack and rest.

After Diego put his things away they took a walk through the beautiful neighborhood, introducing Diego to friends they met along the way. He noticed that Aloha seemed to know her way everywhere they went, and when Kimberly Louise mentioned the marina, Aloha turned and headed in that direction.

"She really does understand a lot, doesn't she, Miss Kimberly Louise?" he asked her.

"Oh yes, she's the smartest dog I've ever seen," said Kimberly Louise proudly.

"Good girl, Aloha! You are the best!" Diego's face flushed with happiness. He was now seeing the result of all of their hard work. Aloha was amazing!

As they climbed back up the steps and reached the porch, Diego collapsed into one of the quaint white rockers. Tyler and Jonathan joined him in other rocking chairs, while David and Kimberly Louise went inside to prepare iced tea.

"Diego, what do you want to be when you grow up?" asked Tyler.

"I think I want to be a doctor, or maybe a vet. What about you?"

"Well, first I'm going to be a dancer, then an astronaut and probably then a lawyer," she replied assuredly.

Diego laughed and turned to Jonathan. "What about you, Jonathan?"

"I want to be a scientist. I really like math and science so my teachers think I'd be good in that field. But first, I think I'd like to raise a guide puppy. The problem is that we don't have any guide dog schools around Atlanta."

"Hey, that might not matter. Why don't you contact some of the guide schools in the east and see if they have puppy raising programs in the Atlanta area?" offered Diego. He sighed and looked pensive. "Sometimes I think about getting another dog and starting all over again."

"So, why don't you?" inquired Tyler.

"Because it's so hard to let them go," answered Diego softly. Just then David returned with a tray of drinks.

"This is another southern tradition," said David, handing Diego a frosted glass of sweetened tea. "You will find it everywhere here, and you're gonna love it as much as we do."

Jonathan told Diego about the beaches and the shrimp boats as they made plans for the week. The soft aroma of summer flowers drifted through the still evening air; Diego realized he was becoming drowsy.

"Perhaps it's time to go inside and rest a little," suggested David. "Diego, what time did you get up this morning?"

"Hmm, I think around five a.m. My folks had to drive me to the airport, and I know it was early."

Aloha stood up from her place at Kimberly Louise's feet and walked over to Diego, placing her head on his knees. She must have known he was ready for bed.

"See you tomorrow, sweet girl," he whispered. "We'll do lots of fun things together as soon as I wake up."

Aloha smiled her goofy grin and returned to Kimberly Louise's chair.

Chapter Twelve

To know what is right and not do it is the worst cowardice.
　　　　　　　　　—Confucius, Chinese philosopher

Diego listened closely as the tour director told them the story of Neptune Small, the antebellum slave who had lived right there on St. Simons Island. At Neptune Park, named in his honor, she explained how he had carried the body of his best friend—his master's son Lordy King—over six hundred miles back to St. Simons Island.

"You see folks, when he was still a young boy, Neptune had promised Lordy's mother, Anna Matilda King, that he would always bring Lordy home. After Lordy was killed in the Civil War, Neptune honored that promise and brought his body back so he could be buried in the family plot. In appreciation, they gave him the most beautiful piece of land on Retreat Plantation to build his own home."

"Nana, how did he bring the body back all that way by himself?" whispered Jonathan.

"I believe he made a carrier from a large piece of deerskin, then attached that to the horse's saddle and pulled it with Lordy's body wrapped up in blankets," answered Kimberly Louise. "You see, Neptune had been given Lordy's horse Bell in Virginia, and he walked her through the dead of winter to get the body back to Georgia."

"Wow! What an incredible story," murmured Diego. He and the others were touched by this story of true friendship between a slave and his master's son.

As they rode around the island on the St. Simons Trolley, Kimberly Louise, Diego, Jonathan and Tyler enjoyed hearing all about the history of the island, as well as the stories about the British General Oglethorpe and how he had founded Georgia, the thirteenth and final colony in the New World.

Aloha lay quietly by Kimberly Louise's feet. When they arrived at old Christ Church, she led her teammate expertly off the trolley. Diego watched proudly, once again thinking about the important role he had played in her early training.

"Your dog is wonderful!" exclaimed a young lady tourist, catching up with them as they made their way through the cemetery at Christ Church. "How old is she?"

"She's just over three." Diego answered quickly, before realizing the question was not directed at him.

Kimberly Louise smiled broadly. "This young man was her puppy raiser, and spent a year and a half preparing her for me," she boasted, placing her hand on Diego's shoulder. "So he deserves a great deal of credit for all of her abilities."

Tyler nodded in agreement. "Yes, and me and my brother Jonathan are Nana's grandchildren. Aloha loves us too, and if I ever go blind like Nana, I'm going to borrow her."

Diego and Jonathan exchanged amused grins. Kimberly Louise laughed happily.

"May I pet her?" asked the young woman, reaching out her hand.

"Nope, not when she's working," answered Tyler, ever alert. She loved being in the middle of conversations.

"But once I stop and she sits down, you may pet her," explained Kimberly Louise, reaching over to gently squeeze Tyler's hand.

As they approached the King family burial plot, Kimberly Louise leaned down to whisper in Tyler's ear.

"Tyler dear, you mustn't answer for others. Remember, *I'm* Aloha's partner so *I'll* let people know when they can pet her. When you are walking her on a leash, then you may decide."

Tyler nodded, looking down at her feet in embarrassment.

The tour guide was pointing out the gravestones of Lordy King and the rest of his family.

"Diego, that's the same man that Neptune walked back over six hundred miles, right?" whispered Jonathan.

"Yes, and here are his brothers and sisters, too. How cool that the whole family is buried right here together!"

They re-boarded the trolley and continued their tour, stopping at Fort Frederica. History unfolded before their eyes as they listened to battle stories and heard about Frederica, the town built by James Oglethorpe to defend the island from the Spanish invasions.

"I wish my parents and Clara could see all this," said Diego. "They'll never believe that I walked through the same woods as the early settlers and Spaniards and the Indians so many years ago!"

"Well, Diego, I say we invite them to come back with you next year," suggested Kimberly Louise. The trolley pulled into the village and Tyler was the first one to jump off.

"There's Miss Mimi! She's here to take us for ice cream!"

"Why Tyler, I don't remember her saying anything about ice cream when she dropped us off," laughed Kimberly Louise. "Do you, Jonathan and Diego?"

"But she will, right Miss Mimi?" insisted Tyler.

"Of course I will, Tyler," she answered, tucking Tyler's small hand into hers. "My favorite flavor is Cookies 'N Cream. What about y'all?"

Aloha lifted her head and sniffed expectantly at the phrase Cookies 'N Cream. Diego laughed, hugging her and promising her part of his cone.

Chapter Thirteen

Fate knows where you are going,
but it is up to you to drive there.
—Michelle Keesling

"Diego, is your backpack ready?" called Kimberly Louise from the kitchen when she heard the doorbell.

"Uh huh, I put it by the front door," he answered. "I'll see who's here."

Kimberly Louise's neighbor Courtney Meyer stood smiling in the doorway. Her dark green bicycle leaned against the lower step.

"Hey, Diego! My brother says you can borrow his bike, but you'll have to go pick it up in our garage."

"No problem. Come in. Maybe you can help Miss Kimberly Louise get the kids ready. Tell her I'll be right back."

He trotted down the street to Courtney's house, whistling

to the beat of his footsteps. David Wells was taking all of them to Jekyll Island to bike and swim. Everyone on St. Simons Island told him that Jekyll Island had the best beaches and they were planning to spend a full day on them. After a picnic lunch, swimming and a bike ride, they would visit the water park, Summer Waves. Diego was mostly looking forward to running on the beach with Aloha.

He had already done so many fun things during the few days he'd spent in Georgia. Just yesterday they had taken the St. Simons Island Trolley Tour, and after lunch at Barbara Jean's Restaurant, Mimi and Kimberly Louise took him inside old Christ Church and showed him the Tiffany stained glass window. Another day they visited the Light House and climbed to the top, enjoying the panoramic view of the island. Everything was new and thrilling to Diego and exploring it with Aloha made it even more wonderful.

Diego had been a little surprised at the sudden change that came over Aloha once the harness was put on her. She still acknowledged him with a wagging tail, but now focused completely on Kimberly Louise. He had learned to expect that in his puppy raising classes, but he still felt pangs of jealousy that he couldn't give her commands or teach her leash training like he had before.

But Diego's jealousy dissolved as he watched the love and bonding between Aloha and Kimberly Louise. And he knew that Kimberly Louise was allowing Aloha to be off harness as much as possible so he could have personal time with her. Aloha's two favorite humans were developing a deep understanding of each other's needs.

David drove into the driveway and Diego helped him load up the bicycles while Jonathan and Tyler packed up the beach gear.

"Hey, y'all. Listen up! Don't tell Kimberly Louise that I've rented a tandem for us to ride," whispered David. "It's a surprise!" Turning to Tyler, he said, "Shhhh."

A moment later Kimberly Louise and Courtney walked down toward them from the house, carrying the picnic basket and cooler and laughing conspiratorially.

"Does everyone have sunscreen on?" asked Kimberly Louise above the clamor of excited voices.

"Yes!" they replied loudly in unison.

Driving across the Jekyll Causeway, Tyler showed Diego and Courtney the exact spot of Kimberly Louise and David's accident over two years ago.

"Right over there," she declared knowingly. "Both cars ended up on that side of the road. One was completely turned over and the other was on its side."

Diego noticed that David stole a glance at Kimberly Louise, but she showed no reaction to her granddaughter's recitation of the event. It made Diego uneasy and he quickly changed the subject.

"Mr. Wells, do you have children?" he wondered.

David smiled into the rearview mirror. "Yes, Diego, I do. They are grown up and live in Maine. My son has two girls, one about your age, and my daughter has one little boy, around seven. Aren't you seven, Tyler?"

"Almost eight," she promptly responded. "When can I meet her?"

"Maybe we can arrange a get-together over the Christmas holidays," offered Kimberly Louise. "Y'all will be here and so will David's family."

"Good. We'll come to Jekyll together and I'll show them where the accident happened," said Tyler. "Hey look, there's Summer Waves!" she cried, as they crested the bridge and the water park loomed off to the right through the veil of pines.

They found a shady spot at Driftwood Beach on the north end of the island. Diego, David and Kimberly Louise set up aluminum tables and chairs while Courtney took the younger ones to the water.

It looked like a tropical island from the movies, framed by long leaf pines and palm trees. White powdery sands gleamed with the late morning sun. Cranes walked gingerly on stilt-like legs, and seagulls were diving for fish. Diego noticed they were surrounded by large gnarled pieces of driftwood, providing shade from the hot sun. He looked over at Aloha and back at Kimberly Louise.

"Miss Kimberly Louise, once we get set up may I take Aloha for a run?" he asked hopefully.

"I wish you would," she said, amused. "She could use one, and I know she won't let you out of her sight."

Kimberly Louise sighed contentedly as she relaxed in her lounge chair. David gently massaged her shoulders with his strong fingers. She turned around, a slow smile spreading across her face.

"Are they all out there having fun?" she asked.

"Indeed they are, and now we can breathe in the salty air and enjoy the gentle lapping of the waves. Just think, sweetheart, we can still have a romantic date even with grandbabies and guests in tow," he chuckled, kissing her tenderly on the crown of her head.

Diego and Aloha raced across the packed sand until they were breathless, collapsing side by side on the sand and watching little sandpipers scamper back and forth at the water's edge. With his arm looped across Aloha's neck, Diego shared his thoughts.

"You know, girl, I was really unhappy when Jeremy's Alma didn't pass the formal guide dog training and he got her back. Remember? Even though he shared her with me, it seemed so unfair that he got to keep his puppy and I lost you." She turned her head to nudge his shoulder, as if she understood.

"And then, when I had to give you up for good to Miss Kimberly Louise, it was even worse. I wanted to scream up there on stage, but I couldn't, because you were going where you needed to go." He paused, reliving that painful memory.

"Now I'm okay with it. I know we'll be in each other's lives, even if it's just for short visits." He hugged her tightly. "Does Miss Kimberly Louise do the things with you that we did: run, throw sticks, and swim long distances?"

Aloha acknowledged the question with her knowing look, and Diego realized that of course they did.

"If I can get her and Mr. Wells to visit us in Oregon, I'll take you back to the rivers we used to swim together. Would you like that?"

Aloha pricked up her ears and smiled her goofy grin. Diego laughed loudly, before turning thoughtful.

"Aloha, I've been thinking about getting another guide puppy. Maybe Clara and I can raise her together. I just feel lonely without you, and that might be a way I can use my skills again. And I know I'll learn a lot too." He ruffled her ears. "Does that sound like a plan?"

Aloha shook her body and looked up at him curiously.

Diego giggled. "O.K., let's go, girl. Let's swim in this nice warm ocean!"

They soon returned dripping wet and covered with sand. The others had already started eating, and Diego lost no time in joining them. He loved the southern deep fried chicken breasts with coleslaw, and asked for seconds on biscuits and green beans. Everything tasted much better at the ocean!

After they cleared away the plates, David led Kimberly Louise over to the tandem bike and lifted her up onto the back seat.

"My dear, we have a surprise for you this afternoon. I know you thought you and Aloha would enjoy an afternoon siesta while the rest of us rode bikes. But we decided you'd rather be in the middle of the fun, so you're going with us!"

Kimberly Louise laughed with delight and gave David a huge hug. He quickly organized the group and lined them up, leaving Aloha free to run alongside. Diego and Courtney, also fourteen years old, led the bikers over the trails.

Jekyll Island's bike paths were amazing, winding from the ocean through the forests, around lakes and golf courses, to the marshes. Then the group turned around and returned by a different route.

"How many miles do you think we rode, Mr. Wells?" asked Courtney after the ride, while they were loading up their bikes in his vehicle.

"I'd say about twelve," he answered. "Wasn't it great?"

"I loved it!" squealed Kimberly Louise. "I hadn't ridden a bike in ages!"

"It was awesome," answered Diego. "The best bike ride

I've ever had! And seeing the buck and two does was so cool!" Aloha sat beside him and he reached down to pet her.

"Hey, little one, are you going on the rides at Summer Waves with us?" he joked.

They spent about two hours at Summer Waves. The four youngsters rushed from one ride to the next, while Kimberly Louise and David enjoyed sweet iced tea and music at the snack shop.

Diego was surprised by how much he enjoyed Courtney's company. They had quite a bit in common, laughing together as they talked about school, friends, and families.

Driving home, Courtney looked over at Diego thoughtfully.

"Diego, my family is going to the Okefenokee Swamp on Friday. Have you ever seen alligators up close? Or been to a swamp?" she asked.

"Not really," he replied.

"Well, if you're not doing anything, why don't you join us? It's really a cool place."

Kimberly Louise broke in. "Go ahead, Diego. You would really enjoy it, and we don't have anything planned for that day."

David reached across the seat for her hand, lightly squeezing her fingers in approval.

Chapter Fourteen

When you have read the Bible, you will know it is the word of God, because you have found it the key to your own heart, your own happiness and your own duty.

—Woodrow T. Wilson

"**O**H MY GOSH! Did you see that?" shricked Diego.

"Yes! It was an eagle diving!" whooped Courtney. She and the others watched breathlessly as a bald eagle swooped down to the river and snatched up a fish.

"Mercy! It's pretty unusual for the tourists to see them fishing right here in the swamp," Jerry the guide pointed out. "Y'all are right lucky, 'cuz even I only see that a couple times a year."

Diego, Courtney and her parents had joined four other tourists on a boat excursion through the Okefenokee Swamp in southern Georgia, one of the oldest and best preserved freshwater areas in America. As their boat glided through the Suwannee River, they saw an old still, remnants of an Indian dugout canoe and several endangered bird species.

"The word Okefenokee means *quivering earth* in the language of the Choctaw Indians," drawled Jerry. "They were here living peacefully among the other Indian tribes for many years; long before the white man arrived and chased 'em all out."

"So, how old is this area?" asked Courtney.

"Over seven thousand years old, I reckon," he answered. "This Suwannee River is the principal outlet for the swamp, and it's two hundred eighty miles long."

Diego wondered about the tea colored water.

"Well now, that's due to tannic acid, which comes from dissolved vegetative material and peat," explained the guide as he steered them expertly through a narrow passage, thick with cypress roots and the gnarled knees of the old trees.

"And how was the swamp formed?" asked Courtney's mother.

"Another good question!" Jerry acknowledged, approvingly. "This here was all part of the ocean floor. Through centuries of erosion and weather, it became a peat-filled bog inside a huge depression. That's what gives us this here swamp y'all see today."

Diego was fascinated with this huge park and had never seen anything like it. They had observed several dozen lazy alligators sunning themselves around the boardwalk near the entrance, their snouts and gleaming red eyes visible above the murky water. Now he spotted another one stretching its long body on the riverbank.

"Hey, I see another alligator! This one's stretching his neck and looking right at us!" he shouted, pointing wildly. Not more than ten feet away, the tourists stared at the twelve-foot alligator with its elongated, lizard-like body and muscular flat tail. Only the teeth of the upper jaw were visible below its broad, dark snout.

"Yah, Ole Sam's got a girlfriend and is checking to see who's approaching his territory," grinned Jerry. "Sometimes we see them fishing together later on in the evening. If you ever come across one on land, run away, zigzagging, as fast as you can!"

The tropical humidity, the wetlands, the stately cypress trees, the exquisite bird sounds, and the pungent aromas of the swamp filled Diego's head. He closed his eyes, hoping to make a memorable visual image.

"Diego, are you okay?" asked Courtney.

He nodded slowly. "I'm fine, Courtney. Just enjoying the Okefenokee Swamp."

"It is amazing, isn't it?" she said, pensive. "I guess we don't appreciate it because it's so close. Kinda like you probably don't appreciate your mountains and snow in Oregon, right?"

Diego laughed. "Yup, I think you're right. That's why I

like to travel. Who would guess back home that all this exists, and right here in the United States!"

Courtney and Diego boarded the train as soon as they finished the boat trip. Riding the short loop around the edge of the swamp, they stopped to visit the remnants of a logging camp, trying to imagine what it would be like living in that place and time.

"You know what, Courtney, I haven't thought once about Aloha until now. I must really be having fun," he said lightly.

"Do you think of her much when you're in Oregon?" she wondered.

"No, just only every once in a while, like when I see other guide dogs. I guess that's pretty good. I wonder how it will be when I go back, since I've been with her for a while now," he mused. "You know, the last few days I've been wondering if I should raise another guide dog. I know my sister would love that, and we could do it together."

"But won't it be hard giving another one up all over again?" she asked.

Diego pulled up several long blades of grass. "Uh huh, and that's what's holding me back. But it's so worth it when you see the results," he mused, thinking of Kimberly Louise. "Then you understand why you did it."

"Will you come back here to see Aloha?" she asked expectantly.

A slow smile spread across his face. "I sure hope so! But now it's my turn to invite them out to visit me in Oregon."

As they drove back to St. Simons Island, Courtney asked the question that had been bothering her.

"Hey Diego. You like it out here, don't you?"

"Sure, it's great. What's not to like?"

"Well, I guess I thought that seeing Aloha again would be hard for you, knowing you'll be leaving her. But it might help if you could bring another puppy out here with you," she suggested.

David smiled. "It's better now, 'cuz I know Miss Kimberly Louise will always let me see her. And I know that Aloha won't ever forget me."

Courtney's face brightened. "Well, maybe I can talk my family into a trip to Portland, Oregon. Then you can show me what your coast is like."

Diego gave a short laugh. "It's cold, lots of waves, and rainy. But you'll like it just fine. Come out whenever you can."

Courtney's parents, overhearing their conversation, smiled and exchanged glances as they pulled into Kimberly Louise's driveway, remembering their own youthful hopes and promises.

Chapter Fifteen

Fear thou not; for I am with thee; be not dismayed; for I am thy God: I will strengthen thee; yea, I will help thee; yea, I will uphold thee with the right hand of my righteousness.

—Isaiah 41:10

"Could you teach me to read Braille?" Diego asked Kimberly Louise.

They had been reading in the sunroom. Diego watched her read and was fascinated with her ability to run her fingers over the dots.

"Would you really like to learn?" She paused, still concentrated on her reading.

"Sure. Is it hard? Why is it called Braille?"

Kimberly Louise finished the page and moved over to the wicker sofa to sit next to Diego.

"It takes time to learn, Diego, but we have time. To answer your question, it was named after a Frenchman, Louis Braille, who accidentally stuck a sharp pointed awl in his eye when he was four years old. The infection spread to his other eye and eventually blinded him in both eyes.

"No longer able to read, at age fifteen he invented a code for himself by punching holes in bits of scrap leather from his father's shop. His system used six dots that corresponded to letters, giving him the ability to read and write an alphabet. Eventually he developed a machine to speed up the cumbersome system."

Diego watched amazed as she demonstrated the system.

"We start with a cell, arranged like the six dots on dice or a domino. Look, it's two vertical rows of three dots each. Each dot has a number. Starting at the left, the top dot is number one. Then reading down the second dot is number two, and the bottom dot is number three. The three dots on the right, starting at the top, are four, five and six."

Soon Diego was trying it out and discovered he was able to form small words.

"This isn't so hard," he pronounced, after practicing almost an hour while Kimberly Louise prepared their dinner.

Tyler and Jonathan had returned to Atlanta the day before, and Diego realized that he missed them. The house seemed strangely silent.

"Miss Kimberly Louise, what is the third eye?" he asked, moving into the kitchen to join her.

She gave him a quick, assessing glance.

"Interesting you should ask that, Diego. We were taught

about the third eye in rehabilitation. It's facial vision. You see with your face, as in feeling something in front of you, or around you. But that's not the only alternative eye we have, you know."

"What do you mean?"

"I mean that we have an eye on the tip of each finger, one at the end of a white cane, one more on the point of each shoe, and one great eye in the center of our brains. You do know that we actually see with our brains, don't you?"

"Even sighted people?" asked Diego.

"Yes. And we feel and hear with our brains too, because it tells us what we are touching and hearing."

"Hmm, so we're sort of like beetles with lots of feelers," suggested Diego.

"That's exactly right! And blind people like me learn to see with our ears, mind and memory."

Diego thought about that. "Then why did you decide to get a dog?"

"Ah hah, good question," she grinned. "I heard that a dog would increase my independence. I knew I'd be lonely, and I was tired of using the white cane. So it all seemed to fall into place at the right time."

Diego pondered that for a few moments. "Miss Kimberly Louise, do you think you and I were supposed to meet each other?"

"I've been told there are no coincidences. Everything that

happens in life has been written long ago. My pastor once said that God drew a circle in the sand exactly around the spot where we are standing right now."

Diego nodded, trying to take it all in.

"I also believe that all of us participate in the manifestations of our own blessings. It's all about giving. If we give something, God will take what we've offered and turn it into something amazing." She paused, reaching up for the dinner plates.

"For example, you gave me the gift of selflessness by raising Aloha and then returning her to Guide Dogs for the Blind. God used your gift to give me a pair of eyes and a loving companion."

Diego gulped, the memory momentarily piercing his heart.

"Do you remember what I told you on the platform during my graduation, Diego? I said you rekindled the spark that went out of my life when I lost my sight. And I also told you that Aloha would now have two masters to love."

She walked over to Diego and put her arms around his shoulders.

"It wasn't up to you to decide how to use your gift of selflessness. The Lord took it and gave it to me in the form of Aloha."

Aloha, knowing they were talking about her, leaned against Kimberly Louise's legs and nudged her wet nose gently into Diego's palm.

"But enough about that . . . now, let's have some ribs," said Kimberly Louise. Aloha pricked up her ears and licked her lips. Food was about to be served, and chances were good that she would get some too.

Chapter Sixteen

Refuse to be average. Let your heart soar as high as it will.
—A.W. Tozer

The breeze was soft and soothing. Diego was swimming at East Beach, enjoying the late August afternoon warmth. Aloha splashed with him in the surf, chasing sticks and an old golf ball she'd found earlier that day. Kimberly Louise sunbathed, her face turned to the sky, her auburn wavy hair tucked under a hat, listening contentedly to the sounds of Diego's laughter. Filled with memories, she pictured the day as a postcard—the perfect meshing of the sea, land and climate.

Diego had been visiting her for eight days. She smiled as she tried to remember the earlier days of summer without him. He seemed to complement her life with his easy-going, cheerful manner. They had shared many delightful moments, and as she spent time with him she understood why Aloha had turned out to be such a giving, sweet dog.

Bottlenose dolphins played in the waves offshore. The

white sand beaches were dotted with joggers and dog walkers. Sandpipers gathered like brown clouds and ran like the wind along the stretch of shell beach. Without warning and as one tightly knit unit, they abruptly changed their direction and scurried off in another direction. Kimberly Louise listened as they took to the air.

"We're back, Miss Kimberly Louise!" panted Diego. He and Aloha landed with a thud at her side.

"Wow! Those are bigger breakers than I've seen before out here! And we just saw two great blue herons wading! When Aloha began to chase them, they bent their long knees and jumped into flight! It was so cool!"

When Aloha heard her name, she rubbed the side of her sandy face against Kimberly Louise's hand and stretched forward to lick her partner's chin. Laughing, Kimberly Louise shifted Aloha's chin to her knee and ran her long fingers through her dog's wet fur.

She felt Aloha stiffen suddenly and raise her muzzle toward the clouds. Kimberly Louise noticed that there wasn't a stirring of air. It was so still and quiet.

"Diego, is there something over there?" she asked. "Aloha is acting odd."

"All I see is that the clouds are moving away quickly and Aloha is watching them go," he replied, following Aloha's intense gaze.

"You know, my senses are extraordinary since I've lost my

sight. I feel the air becoming heavier, and our voices seem to be hanging in suspended animation. Look up, Diego. Is there a change in the color of the sky?"

Diego stared upward. He saw scud clouds moving quickly through an eerily pale glow. Aloha whimpered softly and nudged Kimberly Louise's leg with her paw.

"It sort of looks like an early sunset, Miss Kimberly Louise. I'd say the color of the sky is a muddy yellow. And it is very still, isn't it?"

"Where are the Flemings? Have they come back from their beach walk yet?" Kimberly Louise decided she wanted to go home and hoped her neighbors had returned.

"Why don't I go look for them and ask them if they're ready to take us home," offered Diego. He sensed both Aloha's and Kimberly Louise's restlessness.

Twenty minutes later they were packed up and heading home.

The moment they walked into her house, Kimberly Louise turned on the television.

Tropical storm Karin is moving from the southwest and appears to be turning east. She has picked up speed over the water and may be headed this way. Unless she again changes course, she is expected to reach northeastern Florida and southeastern Georgia sometime tomorrow. Stay tuned for weather bulletins.

Diego glanced out the window. The sun had ducked out of sight and the sky was once again crowded with clouds. There was not a whisper of breeze in the deepening purple sky. The palm trees stood stiff and silent.

"Miss Kimberly Louise, do you think we'll have a hurricane?" he asked in wonder.

Spurts of rain and sudden whirls of wind broke the silence. Diego watched a squirrel as it scurried inside a hole in a live oak tree; birds flew into the thick shrubbery.

"I don't know, Diego. But I do know we're in for a storm. Let's call David and see if he can help us board up the windows."

By evening, David and Diego had hammered plywood sheets over each of Kimberly Louise's lower windows and two of the upper ones, boarded up the garage and porches, and brought in the lawn furniture. They checked the pantry for food and organized Kimberly Louise's important documents into a portable file. Then they sat back to wait.

Over the tops of the beautiful homes on St. Simons Island, the residents watched the sea turn bottle green under a charcoal sky, with slanting lines of incoming rain spreading to engulf the horizon. Along the tree-studded streets of Hampton Point, the palm fronds, battered by a steady north wind, all pointed in one direction—south.

The sky was alive. Lightning scribbled on the dark clouds that had buried St. Simons Island. Thunder shook the earth.

It was as if a curtain had been drawn across the sea—revealing the awesome beauty of a natural disaster seen from above. Huge breakers rolled into the Hampton River from the sea and rumbled through the tributaries. The Atlantic Ocean suddenly had become a seething, moving mass of rolling and thundering waves.

The television gave new advice.

Fill your bathtubs with water to use for drinking or bathing. Tie down anything outside that could become a flying missive, or bring it inside. Women in their final term of pregnancy should head for a hospital nearby, because the huge drop in barometric pressure we are expecting often triggers premature labor.

For the next hour Diego, David and Kimberly Louise sat in front of the television set, searching for storm updates. Finally, they decided the best thing to do was go to bed.

"I'm sure we'll have a better idea tomorrow morning, Diego. And we're prepared for whatever comes. Mimi thinks this could just be a grand adventure, and she reminded me that we've not had a hurricane in this part of Georgia for over one hundred years."

"A real hurricane? Wow! At least it's more exciting than most summer vacations have been for me," he answered, leaning forward to scratch Aloha's head. "I can't wait to call Jeremy and tell him all about it!"

After David left, Aloha stood up and nudged Kimberly Louise into her bedroom. She knew it was bedtime and was looking forward to the soft comfortable bed she shared with her partner, even though she was not completely at ease with the weather outside.

Chapter Seventeen

Worry does not empty tomorrow of its sorrows;
it empties today of its strength.

—Corrie Ten Boom

iego slept soundly that night, exhausted from a day of body surfing and chasing after Aloha. Kimberly Louise slept fitfully, awakening each time Aloha moaned, turned, or grunted with pleasure as she stretched her back legs.

Kimberly Louise listened to the pounding rain and rumbling thunder. In her mind's eye, she was watching the forks of lightning stabbing at the horizon.

The howling wind and driving rain woke Diego up. Thunder crashed and boomed as he stepped sleepily from his bed.

Aloha, sensing that he was up, crept upstairs and into his room, head bent and tail tucked between her legs. Diego called to her and she dove into his arms, almost knocking him over.

"Are you scared, *muchachita*? I remember when loud noises frightened you as a puppy," he murmured, kissing her face and rubbing her neck.

Together they walked into the kitchen, where Kimberly Louise sat drinking coffee and listening to the television news broadcast.

The tropical storm that had threatened from a distance was now making its way slowly up the coast of Florida directly toward Georgia. The announcer had new warnings.

Evacuation is voluntary at this point for residents of coastal Georgia. If Tropical Storm Karin continues on course and becomes a category three hurricane, it will become mandatory to evacuate eight hours before landfall. Storm surge has been anticipated at four feet. Hurricane winds are predicted by 4:00 p.m. this afternoon. Winds are expected at 80 to 85 miles an hour. Stand by for instructions.

"Good morning, Diego. Did you sleep well?" asked Kimberly Louise, covering her yawn with the back of her hand.

"I guess, but these news updates don't sound good. Are you worried?"

"I was thinking we should talk to Mimi and David about evacuating. I'd like to be out of here before we need to be. Oh, and why don't you phone your parents and give them an update? They may be watching the news."

Diego grinned. "I've already done that, Miss Kimberly Louise. I talked to them last night on my cell phone and they reminded me to think about everything I learned when I wrote my school paper on hurricanes. I have most of it memorized, so maybe I can answer questions for you, " he added humorously.

They were interrupted by a knock on the door. Their neighbor Courtney stood dripping wet and grinning at the door.

"Hey, my mom wondered if you needed anything. She let me use her giant umbrella to walk over, but it did no good. I brought her cell phone in case yours doesn't work," she added. "It's really windy and things are blowing all over outside."

"Thanks, Courtney. We're doing okay so far. Aloha is very nervous and I think she needs to go outside to do her business, right girl?" Diego looked down at Aloha's upturned face.

Kimberly Louise was already dialing Mimi's number. "Yes, Diego, please take her out. I'm going to make arrangements with Mimi and David to leave the island before evacuation becomes mandatory."

Diego attached Aloha's leash to her collar and grabbed a large umbrella. "I'll walk you back to your house, Courtney, and we can take Aloha to do her business at the same time."

They stepped outside into gale-force winds that tossed

torrents of rain at them, punching them sideways and rattling windows. The palm trees bent and thrashed in a wild dance. Both umbrellas rapidly blew inside out. Diego grabbed Courtney's arm and they huddled together, cautiously searching for a sheltered place for Aloha. The dog pressed nervously into their legs as if their presence offered protection. Her large dark eyes shimmered with distress.

In the distance they heard choppy waves hammering the seawall. They watched a complaining gull challenge the wind and lose.

Rolling thunder crashed and moaned. Aloha cowered and whimpered, refusing to move. Diego handed Courtney the leash as he bent down to speak with her.

"It's okay, girl. I'm right here with you. You can do this, and then we'll go right back home," he encouraged, holding her head in his hands.

Fingers of lightning jabbed the distant sky. They listened as the river heaved, twisted and smashed into the jetty. The wind whacked the palm leaves together.

They started out again, walking toward a sturdy oak tree. Aloha struggled to walk, wide-eyed and apprehensive, throwing fearful glances over her shoulder at Diego.

Another crackling line of lightning leapt out from above, smashing into a small pine and snapping it in half. Aloha yelped shrilly in pain as a jagged branch swiped her leg. Startled, she jerked the leash from Diego's hand and bolted into the slashing rain.

Diego struggled to propel himself into the wind, shouting her name as he ran after her.

"Come back, Aloha! Here girl, here Aloha," he cried out, drenched, moving slowly forward through the deluge.

Courtney followed him and tried to grab his rain jacket. "What happened, Diego? I think Aloha got hurt!" she whimpered, hot tears coursing down her cheeks.

Finally Diego stopped. The rain was too thick for them to follow Aloha.

"We have to go back to your house!" shouted Diego, struggling to be heard over the booming thunder.

They stumbled back to Courtney's house, where Diego tried to phone Kimberly Louise, but the line was busy. Diego told Courtney's parents about Aloha's disappearance and they immediately offered to help him look for her.

"Thanks, but it's really hard to even walk out there now. I'm sure she'll come back when it lets up a little," said Diego hopefully.

Fighting the storm as he returned to Kimberly Louise's home, Diego prayed. He asked for the right words to comfort her when he explained how Aloha had escaped. Disheartened and afraid, he asked for strength and courage. But most of all, he prayed that Aloha would return as soon as possible.

Meanwhile, Aloha was crouched against the covered corner of a neighbor's dock. Facing away from the wind, she kept her head over her front paws, silently suffering the lashing from the whipping leaves of a nearby palmetto.

Chapter Eighteen

And under His wings shalt thou take refuge.
—Psalm 91:4

A blast of rain and warm wind filled the house as Diego struggled to close the door behind him. "Miss Kimberly Louise, she's gone! She got scared and pulled the leash out of my hand!" He ran to her side, hugging her tight around the waist.

"Oh, Diego, I'm so glad you are back. I was worried about . . ."

"BUT I'VE LOST ALOHA," sputtered Diego, holding back sobs. "And I think she may be hurt, too. I'm so sorry, Miss Kimberly Louise." Diego burrowed his face into her shoulder. She held him while he cried, refusing to let her mind process his news. After a while she spoke.

"Thank God you are safe, Diego dear. Aloha can take care of herself. Come, let's sit down and you tell me what happened."

While Diego was explaining what happened to Aloha, Kimberly Louise was nervously checking off her options. Mimi had promised to come by for them in an hour. David would be leaving in the evening and could pick them up. But Kimberly Louise knew she had to stay in her home until Aloha returned.

"Listen closely, Diego. Mimi will come by for us in an hour. You should go with her and get off the island. I must wait here until Aloha returns. I'm sure I can talk David into staying with me."

"NO! I'm not going to leave Aloha here either! I'm waiting with you. I'm gonna be your eyes until she comes back," he insisted, battling a wave of helplessness.

"Then that's what we'll do," decided Kimberly Louise. "I want you to tell me everything you know about hurricanes, right after I let Mimi know she'll have to leave us behind."

Mimi, Kimberly Louise and David agreed that Mimi would leave and David could pick them up later. They convinced themselves that Aloha would have found her way back by then. They had confidence in her intelligence and amazing sense of direction.

"So, let's talk about what we're facing here. But first, I want to share with you a phrase that I've always held close to my heart." She sat down and patted the couch next to her.

"When I was agonizing after being told I'd never see again, a kind, compassionate doctor told me something I'll never forget: *the only place the mind will ever find peace is inside the silence of the heart. That's where you need to go.*"

Diego nodded solemnly.

"You too, Miss Kimberly Louise."

"Yes, we'll both go there and ask the Lord to guide Aloha home," she concurred.

Diego looked at Aloha's empty harness propped against the wall and flinched.

"Now, Diego, tell me all about hurricanes," suggested Kimberly Louise.

Diego tried to mimic her light mood. But his heart was heavy as he struggled to let go of his fear for Aloha.

Moving to sit on a chair across from her, he began. "O.K., well, do you know what a hurricane is?"

"I know a little about hurricanes, but you tell me," answered Kimberly Louise.

"Well, in the summer months, when the ocean is warm from being in the sun all day, it heats the air above it. This warm air is lighter than the air around it, so it rises—just like bubbles in boiling water. These air bubbles get bigger because there's less pressure. They also get colder, and make the water vapor in the air condense into droplets. Does that make sense?" asked Diego.

"Yes. You're doing a great job of making me visualize it," smiled Kimberly Louise.

"After water vapor condenses, heat is left over. This heat

raises the bubbles until they build up the towering cumulus clouds, which form a thunderstorm. When a couple of thunderstorms get together, each one releases enough energy to keep the others going, and a hurricane is formed. So a hurricane is really a big cone of whirling air, spiraling upward like smoke. And hurricane winds curve and whirl until they make a circle, traveling as fast as two hundred miles an hour."

"O.K., Diego. I have a picture in my mind of a top spinning across the floor. Isn't a hurricane like that: spinning around and traveling forward at the same time?"

"Uh huh. That's a great description, Miss Kimberly Louise," Diego nodded.

"Diego, you sound like a scientist. You must have really enjoyed researching this, and you've learned it well," commented Kimberly Louise.

"Thanks." Diego was surprised he remembered so many details from his term paper.

Outside, a booming clap of thunder seemed to shake the house.

"And thunder is the sound of air expanding, after the lightning heats it up," added Diego.

"What about the wind?" asked Kimberly Louise. "Did you research that also?"

"Uh huh. Wind happens when air from a high-pressure area pushes into an area of low pressure, trying to equalize the two. When there's a big difference between the areas, the winds are more violent. And there's no pressure to slow the winds down over the ocean so they start to blow even stronger."

"Amazing! Now tell me, Diego. Do you know why it's called a hurricane?"

"Yes I do. That was part of my report too. In 1495, on his second voyage to the New World, Columbus was hit by a hurricane. The native Caribbean Indians warned the Spaniards that their god *Huracán* was going to strike, so Columbus found safety in Hispaniola and rode out the storm. But he still lost two of his ships. Later, *huracanes* were called *hurricanes* in English."

"Diego, I'm so proud of you. Now I know more about hurricanes than I've ever even imagined, and we are experiencing one to boot!" smiled Kimberly Louise.

"But we don't have Aloha, and we can't do anything about getting her back," said Diego, casting his eyes downward. "Miss Kimberly Louise, would you pray with me for her return?"

"Of course, Diego. I'll pray first." She bowed her head. "Oh Lord, we are trying to be brave and show good faith, but our hearts are crying out for our sweet Aloha. If it is Your will, could You please bring her back to us, safe and sound? Our possessions and the house are only material things, but our safety and Aloha's is what really matters."

Diego, comforted by her words, remained thoughtful and still. After several moments, he cleared his throat and began.

"Dear God, I lost Aloha in the storm and I can't forgive myself. But You can forgive me. So I'm asking You to bring her back here, so she can be Miss Kimberly Louise's partner again. I'm going to try and be brave and trust You to please answer our prayers. Amen."

"And you know that He always hears our prayers, right Diego?"

He nodded. Kimberly Louise rose from the couch. "Now let me go and find us some lunch."

Diego felt better. He almost convinced himself that Aloha would come back to them soon.

Chapter Nineteen

Be thou the rainbow in the storms of life.
The evening beam that smiles the clouds away,
and tints tomorrow with prophetic ray.

—Lord Byron

The harsh tone of the telephone pierced the temporary silence in the house. Diego picked it up and handed it to Kimberly Louise.

"Kimberly Louise, can you hear me?" Mimi, hearing a loud crash as something slammed into the side of Kimberly Louise's home, yelled into the phone. The driving rain was pelting the windowpane as Mimi strained to hear.

"Yes, Mimi, where are you?" Kimberly Louise shouted over the booming wind.

"Listen closely, Kimberly Louise. DO NOT leave St. Simons Island. Move upstairs to your guest bedroom away from the window and stay indoors."

"Don't leave? David just called that he's coming to pick us up. What's wrong?"

"Part of the Torras Causeway is under water and the cars driving on it are floating away. You can't leave now! I've just spoken to David and told him not to leave either. He says he'll phone you and come by to check on you as soon as he can."

"Where are you?" hollered Kimberly Louise. Trembling, she reached for Diego's hand.

"I'm headed for Waycross and . . ." The phone went dead.

Kimberly Louise dialed Mimi's cell phone, but there was no connection. When she tried to dial David's number, she discovered she no longer had a dial tone.

"Diego, my phone is dead! Try yours," she pleaded.

Diego pulled out his mobile phone. There was no signal.

"What did Mimi say?" he asked, sitting down beside her.

Kimberly Louise sank down on the couch. "We can't leave now. The bridges are covered with water," she sighed. Although she understood the danger they would face on the flat open causeway, her fear of staying here was interfering with her ability to reason.

Another blast of thunder shattered the air.

"We have to take blankets, candles, flashlights and containers of water upstairs as quickly as possible," directed Kimberly Louise. "Also, please go to the pantry and bring up some food," she added. "I'm going to get my personal things. Go get yours too."

Diego glanced out the window and saw the dark water rising around the house as the river spilled over its banks. *Poor Aloha*, he thought. *How can she possibly make it through this?* He stifled a sob rising up in his throat.

Outside the wind bellowed like a mad animal howling to get in. The lights flickered and went out and they were thrown into darkness. The house fire alarm sounded with its deafening, robotic *beep-beep-beep*.

Now there would be no air conditioning or fans, and soon the house would become unbearably hot. As they made their way upstairs with their meager supplies, they had to walk through water leaking into the house under the front door.

Their radio still worked. Listening between the screeching static, they were able to keep up with the storm's progress.

Get to a confined space: a place with no windows in case of airborne debris. Hurricane Karin is currently a mid-category three, but unfortunately, she has warmer coastal water to cover. With the storm surge, flooding can occur up to six miles inland, with complete inundation of our barrier islands.

Unexpected tears speckled Kimberly Louise's cheeks as she walked around the room, helping Diego move the guest beds away from the window. She knew they had to keep away from the water because of lightning. As they worked, distant lightning strikes lit up objects in the room through the highest window; lightning they both could hear but only Diego could see.

Kimberly Louise silently prayed for Aloha's safety. She knew how worried Diego was, and how guilty he felt about taking Aloha outside, so she was careful not to let him know how frightened she felt. Instead, she proposed playing a card game.

"Diego, come here. Let's sit down and play cards. I have decks in Braille and written letters," she suggested hopefully.

Diego agreed, knowing he needed to be distracted, if only for a short period of time. For the next hour, they relaxed enough to ignore most of the outside noises. Diego barely noticed the darkness as night fell, since the afternoon had been gloomy and the boarded windows allowed very little light to enter the house.

They broke up the game and ate their cold dinner, each avoiding the subject of Aloha. It was just too painful to verbalize their fears for her and the remote chance of her making it back through the hurricane.

"I think I need to rest a bit, Diego. How about you?" asked Kimberly Louise, wrapping herself in a sheet and lying down on one of the twin beds.

"Yeah, I'll just read a little while, and then go to sleep," he answered.

Soon they were both sound asleep, enjoying temporary relief from the storm.

Chapter Twenty

*It is not because things are difficult that we do not dare,
it is because we do not dare that they are difficult.*

—Lucius Annaeus Seneca

The booming sound of thunder crashed through the walls. The wind was howling, a slow continuous roar that rose and fell. Without warning the wind rushed inside the house through a small hole in the ceiling, lifting small objects around the room. Glass shattered as blasts of rain beat on the countertops below and the house shuddered under the wind's ceaseless pummeling. Diego and Kimberly Louise leaned against the closet wall and held on to each other.

Through the worsening static on the radio, Kimberly Louise and Diego pieced together the news.

As clocked by the reconnaissance plane, winds from Hurricane Karin have risen to 131 miles an hour, with gusts up to 200 miles. We are now experiencing between six to twelve inches of rain per hour, and the surge could measure ten to twelve feet. This is rapidly becoming a Category Four hurricane. Stay indoors and seek high ground!

After a while Diego walked to the window and watched in amazement as flimsy wooden shingles blew by. He wondered if they were from Kimberly Louise's house or someone else's. He turned his head when she spoke.

"Diego, I'm so worried about Aloha. Where could she be and how can she possibly survive this?" whimpered Kimberly Louise, wiping at her eyes and nose. Fear, warm and watery, rushed through her body.

"But you know how smart she is. She's a great swimmer and her sense of smell will bring her back to us when it's safe," answered Diego, trying to sound more reassuring than he felt. "Or someone will find her and bring her home after it's over."

They listened to angry waves slapping somewhere under the window. Peering down from the upstairs window, Diego focused his flashlight on the lawn, noting with despair that everything was under water.

A loud buzzing noise like an angry insect pierced the silence.

"What's that sound, Diego?" whispered Kimberly Louise, flinching involuntarily.

"There's some slits in the roof and I think insects are looking for protection here in the house," answered Diego.

His eyes searched the room and he gasped. Partially hidden behind the dresser's thick leg about two feet in front of him, Diego could barely recognize the form of a snake, its tail raised and coiled for the strike. The snake had the markings of a Canebreak Rattlesnake, gray with an orange stripe running down its back. Diego knew the warning of the rattles meant: "*stay away or I'll strike.*"

"Don't move, Miss Kimberly Louise," he whispered.

But she turned abruptly, stepping closer to the sound of Diego's voice and just missing the rattlesnake by inches.

Her rapid movements told the rattler that she was the enemy. Diego watched horrified as the snake uncoiled and lunged. Time seemed to stand still.

Kimberly Louise let out a soft moan as she felt a sharp, piercing pain scalding her leg. Tears welled in her eyes and a wave of nausea swept over her as the snake's fangs sank in.

"Diego, what happened?" she cried out, sinking to the bed.

Diego watched mesmerized as the snake pulled back its head and flicked its tongue in and out. The rattler's forked tongue waved up and down in slow motion like a banner, cautiously seeking a way to escape. Its body flowed softly to the right, hesitated, and finally slithered out through the open doorway to safety, exiting the same way it entered.

"Please Diego, tell me why I'm hurting," she pleaded.

Diego snapped back to reality, looking down at the two

puncture wounds on her leg, about one inch apart. Several tiny drops of blood seeped from the wounds.

"Oh my gosh, Miss Kimberly Louise. You were just bitten by a rattlesnake, and I was watching it disappear. What should we do?" he asked.

"Dear Lord, a rattlesnake?" she gasped. "Diego, are you sure?"

"Yes, a Canebreak rattler. I know its markings. It wasn't too big so I think it's young and probably didn't have much venom." He shook his head, forcing his mind to clear. "O.K., try to stay calm. Do you have a snakebite kit?" Diego was wracking his brain to remember his Boy Scout training on poisonous snakes.

"Yes, downstairs in my bathroom in the first-aid kit. It's in a bright yellow box. I wonder . . ."

Diego interrupted her.

"Lay down on the bed, Miss Kimberly Louise. I'll get the first-aid kit," he said.

Carrying his flashlight and making his way carefully down the stairs through the rising water, Diego fought hard to keep from being sucked toward the door. Slammed against the wall, he watched in horror as Miss Kimberly Louise's china cabinet shattered and collapsed, scattering delicate glass and crystal objects onto the waterlogged carpet. He recoiled and lost his footing as a crackling line of lightning leaped out of the blackness above and hurled into the roof.

Steadying his hand on the floor as he searched for his flashlight, Diego shuddered when his fingers encountered strange pieces of debris floating in the dirty water. Wincing in disgust, he envisioned the bushy rough object that bumped into his arm as a dead rat. Snatching up his flashlight, drenched and useless, he practically gagged as he released it back into the water.

Hurry, hurry! Diego repeated to himself, fighting his way through the murky water to her bathroom. *There isn't much time left before the venom poisons her!*

Trying desperately to remember the procedure for venomous snakebites he had memorized long ago, Diego felt his mind whirling and disoriented. *Just keep her calm. Don't let the poison travel quickly because of a fast-beating heart.*

Gulping deep breaths as he felt his way through the darkened bathroom door, Diego's wet fingers fumbled through the first-aid kit until he found the Sawyer Snakebite Kit, dry and intact. Squinting to read the small letters, he saw that it contained folded instructions, antiseptic pads in foil, and a syringe-like suction device to be applied directly to the fang puncture sites. He read the directions under the dim outside light as he staggered through a whirling mist of angry wind pushing inward through the leaking roof. It felt so surreal; as if he were in a dream.

Once back in the bedroom, he slid a blanket under her shoulders and explained what he was doing over the noise of

117

the rolling thunder. "It's important to slow the flow of venom and remove as much as I can, so I'm going to clean your wound and follow the instructions in the kit. Just lay completely still."

Diego set to work. He quickly fitted the clear plastic adapter to the Sawyer vacuum device, allowing its vacuum to cover both fang marks simultaneously. Applying pressure and working the suction, he saw a brief increase in the red blood seepage from the paired fang wounds. As he worked he noticed that the area was already swelling and beginning to turn a strange color.

Then a frightening thing happened. The bleeding suddenly stopped! *Oh my gosh! It's not going to work. I've done something wrong!* Diego panicked and gripped a chair to steady himself.

A moment later a thick yellow-green fluid began oozing from the wounds into the suction chamber. Just a little bit came out at a time, but it flowed steadily.

"Venom, venom! That's what it is," murmured Diego. "My Scout Master taught us the color. Thank God! I'm doing the right thing!"

Glancing worriedly back at his friend as he worked, he noticed her eyes were closed and her face seemed unusually pale. Her red hair was damp with perspiration, but she was breathing slowly, in and out. He took that as a good sign. At least she wasn't hyperventilating.

He shuddered when he looked at her leg. It was swollen, and had a mottled look—white, grey, and pale blue. When he touched it lightly, it twitched.

"Are you all right, Miss Kimberly Louise?" he asked disheartened. She heard him vaguely, as if through a heavy cloud, and felt as if she were watching both of them from above. She smiled and nodded weakly.

With a great summoning of courage, Diego prayed. *Dear God, help me to do the right thing. Please save Miss Kimberly Louise. I'm all she has left here to protect her. Please God. I'm counting on you. And please bring back Aloha safely. Amen.*

As he reached for her hand, he felt a tear of frustration rolling down his cheek, and swiped at it angrily. From somewhere in the back of his mind he remembered his Scout Master's words: *Being brave isn't being unafraid. It's doing something even though you are afraid.*

Concentrating through sheer will, Diego continued working the suction device until he saw no more venom coming through. Although it seemed to take forever, Diego read on the face of his watch that only forty minutes had passed.

Kimberly Louise seemed to be sleeping now. Diego stood up and wiped his brow.

A moaning sound escaped from her throat, an involuntary keening. In her dreamlike state she felt fire burning in her leg.

Diego sat back down and took a deep breath.

Miss Kimberly Louise mumbled and slowly rolled her head back and forth on the pillow, moving her lips as if she were trying out different words in her head. Diego had to lean close to her mouth to understand her.

"If somethun' goes wrong, you did yur best," she murmured, her tongue thick and dry.

Diego paced restlessly around the two beds and over to the window, repeating her words in his head. *She's not going to die! I won't let her!* The wind roared more loudly, and Diego thought the little house sounded like the inside of a train tunnel. More wooden shingles ripped off the other houses and blew past the window. He had never felt so afraid in his life; not when they had lost Aloha while he was her puppy raiser, or even yesterday when she ran away.

Diego stood rigidly and watched small trees being ripped out by their roots. Logs swirled past the house, and through the moving waters Diego saw dead fish floating on the top, eyes empty and unseeing.

He turned to study Miss Kimberly Louise, sleeping fitfully. But she was breathing smoothly and he thought the unusual color of her leg was fading slightly. Diego wanted to believe that removing the venom had saved her life and she was going to be fine.

Swirls of Technicolor crossed Kimberly Louise's closed eyes and drifted away, carrying her with them. Her increasingly out-of-order brain began imagining shimmering visions. When she attempted to speak to Diego, she noticed her mouth was unable to move with her voice.

She finally decided it was all too much of a strain, and urged her body to float far away from the room.

Chapter Twenty-One

It's not the size of the dog in the fight.
It's the size of the fight in the dog.
—Mark Twain

Aloha was struggling to breathe. Sleet-like wind and rain slapped her face, stinging her eyes, forcing her to turn away from the wind. She fought to keep afloat—soaked, cold and pelted by the relentless storm.

She battled the angry river to swim toward the house. But with each stroke the current carried her further away from Kimberly Louise. Captured by the current, she was dragged under again and again. She tried grabbing onto floating pieces of wood but couldn't get a grip.

An undertow—a sucking, sweeping backwash—took her further away from the shore. Up, then down, slammed with spray, ripped inward, then shoved out. She kicked hard. A strong tide tugged at her hindquarters. Branches and other obstacles loomed up in front of her and banged against her heaving sides and injured leg.

The wake tide caught her and sucked her under again, spinning her body around and around before she could fight clear of it. Her lungs were almost bursting. With her mouth and throat full of water, Aloha fought and splashed in a delirium of terror. The hurricane's roiling clouds seemed like an avalanche bearing down on her.

When she finally surfaced, sputtering and panting, she gasped for just enough breath to fill her lungs. Her groping forepaws felt the impact of a submerged rock, and with her last ounce of strength she crawled feebly onto a narrow sand spit, where she collapsed and laid shivering, panting, and struggling for breath.

Her legs were wobbly, but in a few minutes she gathered enough strength to stagger away from the foaming, pounding waves. The land seemed to have been devoured by the surf. Ocean and river debris lay everywhere: twisted metal, broken wood, shells, downed trees, tires and boats. The palm trees bent forward, flailing their fronds as they touched against the ground and shaking like rag dolls.

After some time Aloha teetered to her feet and sniffed, turning her head from side to side. Her sensitive nostrils quivered at the aromas that enveloped them. Nothing was familiar. She was nowhere near her home, and couldn't detect Kimberly Louise's scent.

Savage, turbulent black clouds whirled toward her and knee-high waves broke just behind her. The foam from the surf had blown into the windward brush, giving it a cotton-coated look. The wind seemed to be growing stronger.

Aloha began to crawl sideways, like a crab. She couldn't stand up straight when she faced and confronted the full blast of the storm, even in the shelter of the trees. Sand and salt stung her face. She recoiled as one small tree leaned toward her precariously. The rising water had loosened its roots and it was unable to withstand the force of the driving rain.

The tree fell with a crash beside Aloha. Small birds like stuffed toys were thrown into the water, some splashing with wildly flapping wings to nearby trees and branches floating by. Others were caught in the branches and disappeared into the waves, or whipped out of sight by the violent wind to their deaths. A gust of wind blowing across the open water shoved her so ferociously that she almost tumbled back into the river.

By bracing her legs and taking slow, deliberate steps, she made her way up a riverbank. Blinking her tired eyes, she saw a large house in the distance. The rain was coming down in slower torrents, and the howl of the wind seemed less dramatic. Aloha reached a small woodshed, nosed her way inside and huddled in the far corner, folding her tail under her paws and pressing her head against them. This protected her from most of the wind and the rain leaking in through the shattered roof.

Aloha slept the deep sleep of the dead and when she awoke

she was bewildered. Her nostrils were aquiver with new odors as she rose to her feet, tense and alert. After shaking herself thoroughly she paused and stood perfectly still, acutely aware of the ache in her right hind leg, where the tree limb had ripped into her flesh. She realized the wind and rain had stopped, and tentatively approached the door.

Light streamed through the door. The ground was cluttered with debris: limbs, entire trees, an occasional dead fish or bird. The sun was shining and the dawn air glowed to a pale yellow. Overhead seagulls cried mournfully.

Aloha stepped out cautiously. She saw a cottage up ahead and limped over to investigate. Carefully placing one foot before the other to climb the stairs, she made it to the door and sat down, whimpering softly. After a few moments, she lifted her paw and scratched. Finally, she let out a yelp and waited for several moments before crying out again.

No one answered her call. She lay down slowly, gathering up her strength. After a short time passed, she lifted up an ear to an unfamiliar sound.

"Well, hello there little one. How did you get here?" asked a friendly voice.

Aloha looked up into a bearded face and cocked her head. The nostrils of her moist black nose twitched sensitively as she sniffed his presence. He reached down to pat her on the head.

"Nobody is staying in this house," he chuckled, "but you can come on over to the lodge and bunk with me. This place is pretty much deserted except for me, the horses, and now you."

Aloha forced herself to her feet and slowly wagged her tail. The man started down the steps with Aloha following closely at his heels. Accompanying the man across the yard, she painfully climbed up more steps to a wide porch and walked into a large building.

Aloha observed her surroundings: large rooms filled with heavy furniture, animal head trophies and racks hanging on the walls, and shards of broken glass all over the floors.

"Be careful, doggy. The hurricane did some damage to our lodge. I don't want you to get cut." He reached down to pick up the glass and noticed Aloha's raw jagged wound, red and coated with sand.

"My goodness, what happened to you? You need some doctoring, my friend," he said as he fingered the tag on her collar. "Aloha is your name, and you're a guide dog," he read, surprised. "Where's your partner?"

He left Aloha in the lodge and hurried outside to look for a boat or a stranded person. Returning to the house after an unsuccessful search, he found Aloha watching and waiting for him by the door.

He laughed and gave her a quick hug. "You must be hungry, Aloha," he said, leading her into the kitchen. "Here's water and some ground meat. I'm afraid I don't have any dog food in here."

When she finished eating, he took out a bottle of hydrogen peroxide and set to work, cleaning out the wound.

"I can't bandage it because you'll just bite it off," he chuckled, "but I'll make sure you don't go out and roll in the mud now that I've fixed you up."

For an hour and a half, Aloha lay beside her new friend's foot, sleeping and listening to the sounds of birds returning and horses whinnying in the distance.

After lunch, he tied a rope around her collar and took her outside to do her business. Looking up at the thick darkening clouds, he grumbled.

"It won't be long now, girl, before the back wall of the hurricane's eye hits us. We'll have to sit this one out together. Then I'll see about getting you back home."

Turning around slowly, he watched the sun—a yellowish-white blur—dim almost completely. The air was shrouded in veils of mists, and the heavier clouds were thickening. Suddenly a bolt of lightning flashed in jagged daggers in front of them. Booming thunder followed, and Aloha and her friend hurried up the stairs to the safety of his large house.

Chapter Twenty-Two

Every accomplishment starts with the decision to try.

—Anonymous

Kimberly Louise moaned, opened one eye and fought her way into misty consciousness. She could hear the shutters softly rattling, and realized that the noise was less intense than before. Before what? When had she last heard the shutters rattling? She wiggled her toes and found she had feeling in them. Her right leg hurt and her mouth was very dry.

Someone had put a water bottle beside her bed. Turning on her side, she felt a lump in the bed next to hers. Was she in the hospital? Slowly and sleepily, she began gathering her thoughts and realized she was upstairs in a guest room in her own house. Diego lay sound asleep on top of the other twin bed.

Outside, the sky was clearing and the sun was shining. Kimberly Louise's confused mind brought back images of the snakebite and the hurricane. The unnatural quiet made the hurricane seem like a distant memory. She had no idea when it had passed, or how long she'd been sleeping.

"Diego, are you awake?" she rasped, in a voice that sounded two weeks old.

There was no answer. She pulled herself up on the bed, swallowed a drink of water and called his name again.

"Huuh, what?" answered the groggy boy, still half-asleep.

"Diego, WAKE UP!" This time she raised her voice as loudly as she could.

"Whaaaat?" Diego jerked upright, checking out the room.

"Diego, it's so quiet. Weren't we just in a hurricane? When did it stop?"

Now Diego was wide-awake. "Oh no! I must have slept all night! I was supposed to be watching you," he groaned, rubbing his eyes. She could feel his anxious eyes shining like a soft heat from a lamp. She didn't blame him for feeling scared.

Stumbling out of bed, he carefully touched her forehead. "How do you feel?"

She reached up for his hand. "I have a terrible headache, and now I remember that a rattler bit my leg. It hurts and stings when I touch it, but it doesn't feel like it's very swollen. How does it look?" she asked hopefully.

Diego examined her leg, and saw that it was no longer as discolored as the day before. Some natural color was returning to the area around the wound, and the swelling seemed to be subsiding.

Looking into her worried eyes, Diego smiled broadly. "Miss Kimberly Louise, you're gonna live! I think I got all the venom out and you'll be fine!" He grabbed her face and planted a loud kiss on her pale right cheek.

She chuckled. "Thank you, Diego. I'm a little nauseous but I'm starving! How long have I been sleeping?"

Diego looked at his watch. "Whoa, about fifteen hours, Miss Kimberly Louise," he calculated. "I don't know when I fell asleep, but the winds were . . . wait a minute," he gulped, hurrying to the window. "What happened to the hurricane?"

Looking through the weatherboards, Diego saw light— sunlight, and felt dry heat, like an oven, coming through the walls. He was perplexed that he didn't hear wind.

"Miss Kimberly Louise, I'll be right back. I'm going outside to see what's happening. Maybe Aloha is at the door crying for us," he called hopefully as he rushed to the stairs, slipping down the soggy bottom stair in his attempt to reach the front door.

Diego's throat closed up when he saw the world of debris that cluttered the yard. Dead fish, birds, trees, limbs, pieces of roofs, parts of boats, and other unbelievable sights lined the streets and gardens. Only the distant slap and hiss of waves spoke of the terrible force unleashed on the island.

He raised his head to discover a light blue sky; he felt he

was inside a large quiet amphitheatre. Was his mind playing tricks on him? He sensed that the world's biggest machine of destruction was centered around him as he stood there, surrounded by calm.

Then Diego remembered his report on hurricanes. He realized they were in the eye of the hurricane, when everything calms down before picking up again. Soon the wind would be blowing even harder from the opposite direction. He shuddered.

"ALOHA, come home, girl. *Ven acá, muchachita.* (Come here, little girl.) WHERE ARE YOU, Aloha?" he screamed into the lull outside, again feeling the unnatural resonance in the air.

Diego waited a few more moments. An involuntary sob shook his body. Heavy-hearted, he turned back to climb the front steps. Just as he reached the door, he heard the sound of an engine.

"Hey Diego, wait up!" called out David, stepping down gingerly from his truck, water surging over his knees when he walked toward Diego.

"Mr. Wells, how did you drive through all this?" asked Diego incredulously.

"Very carefully," chuckled David, grabbing several bags of groceries from the other side. "This truck has big tires, but it still wasn't easy."

Turning to Diego, he asked, "How are you two doing? I

came over as soon as I could and packed up my food supplies to share with y'all."

"I'm so glad you're here," Diego remarked truthfully. "Miss Kimberly Louise was bitten by a rattler, and now she's . . ."

"WHAT? Is she all right?" David's voice rose in alarm.

"Yes, she seems fine. I used her first-aid kit and removed the venom, and she slept all night. But the worse news is that Aloha is gone!" he groaned.

"What do you mean *gone*?" gasped David.

"I took her outside during the storm and she broke away when a tree branch hit her leg. We can't find her and don't know if she's dead or alive." Diego was shocked by the brutal sound of his own words. He had finally voiced the possibility that he and Kimberly Louise had feared all along.

"But thank God you're here to help us!" said Diego, relief flowing through his body.

Kimberly Louise heard voices as they climbed the stairs. "Diego, who's there with you?" she called from the bedroom.

"Hello sweetheart! I've come to feed you and take care of you!" announced David, stopping momentarily at her door. "May I come in?"

Kimberly Louise was overjoyed to see David and reached out to him. After their prolonged embrace, he gave her two Tylenols and gently lifted her head to help her swallow them. He cleaned her wound with an antiseptic pad and bathed her forehead with cool water. Finally he sat down next to her, holding her weak body in his strong arms.

The three of them ate their cold breakfast of muffins, fruit, juice and cereal. David had bought more provisions, knowing that the eye of the hurricane would soon pass and the hurricane would return in full force. Although no one mentioned Aloha by name, her presence seemed to fill up all the air in the house, touching their hearts like a warm breeze.

Chapter Twenty-Three

*Thou shall forget thy misery, and remember it
as waters that pass away.*

—Job 11:16

Diego stretched and walked over to the window. "It's too dark for noon. Everything is covered with mist. And a breeze is starting up again. I think it's coming back," he noted, watching the low thick clouds forming.

The wind increased—a slow continuous roar that rose up and grew louder. A bolt of lightning flashed in jittering daggers over the water. Thunder crashed over the silent skies, followed by sheets of rain. Diego's eyes were fixed on a scattering of gulls shrieking past overhead.

"Listen to it!" exclaimed David. "A hurricane has a sound, a beat, like no other wind: *boom, swish, boom, swish.*"

Kimberly Louise nodded slowly. "I'll tell you what it sounds like to me. I can picture a big elephant caught in a fence. I hear her *swish, swish* with her trunk and *pound, pound* with her feet, fighting to be free."

They passed the time playing cards and reading, while outside rains slammed into the house like crashing waves. Water surged in under the doorways and through the chinks in the weatherboards, but they stayed dry, sheltered in the small upstairs bedroom. From time to time, one of them tried unsuccessfully to communicate on their mobile phones.

"Do you think the winds are up to one hundred thirty miles an hour?" asked Diego, laying down his cards and pacing the room again. "I think that would make Karin a Category Four Hurricane."

"We'll know when it's all over and we get our power back," said Kimberly Louise. Their battery-run radio had died, leaving them without any news.

"At least the rains have cooled the air," David said, moving next to Kimberly Louise and picking up her hand. "It's not too bad even up here without air-conditioning or fans."

"Let's each guess how much rain has fallen," suggested Kimberly Louise. "The winner gets a prize."

"O.K., I'm going to say thirty inches," volunteered Diego.

"That's a good guess, Diego. I'll say thirty-five. What about you, Kimberly Louise?"

"Hmm, I'll go for fifty inches by the time this is all over."

"And what will the prize be?" asked Diego, without missing a beat.

"How about a trip to the Jacksonville Zoo?" suggested Kimberly Louise. "The losers pay the winner's ticket. If you lose, Diego, you can pay with clean-up chores I'll need you to do around here. Is that a deal?"

"Deal," they agreed.

Downstairs, black murky water rose another few inches inside the house. They listened as one more glass window shattered below.

David stood up. "I once read that a hurricane is like a ballerina, with long and elegant arms stretching for hundreds of miles, embracing all within her reach. And her fury—the waves, the wind, the lightning, the rain—are all choreographed to create awe. Like God, she holds life and death in her hands."

"David, that's depressing." Kimberly Louise frowned as she shuffled the cards and put them away. "I say we all close our eyes and rest." She was tiring quickly and her leg ached.

The winds were blowing from the opposite side of the hurricane's eye now, just as furiously as before, but traveling northeast to southwest. Trees already blown down were lifted up momentarily, and then thrown down in the other direction.

They slept. David woke up first, and noticed it was seven p.m. Something had changed. He crept to the window, quietly and cautiously, and looked out.

Without any warning it had stopped. The rain slackened into a wind-whipped sprinkle, and the sky lightened. Once again, the sky was cloudless and still and the wind sounded like a forlorn whimper. The hurricane had passed.

As if on cue, both Diego and Kimberly Louise opened their eyes.

"Stay here and rest, dear," whispered David to Kimberly Louise. Turning to Diego, he spoke.

"Come on, Diego. Let's check downstairs and outside and then we'll report what we see."

Once again they waded through the black water and debris. Each held his breath as David opened the door; each wanting to see Aloha sitting on the porch. The already-saturated lawn was littered with more tree limbs, boat parts, animals, birds and shingles. Rubble and garbage floated through the streets.

At least the heat had broken. For a moment after the downpour the land became fresh, almost sweet smelling. A rainbow blessed the southeast sky.

As they stood outside, concentrating on the horizon, the sun broke through the sky. And with the sun came the humidity; the air thickened until it became an oppressive mush, bringing forth the unpleasant odors of destruction.

"Should we even call her?" asked Diego.

David looked into Diego's discouraged eyes. "She'll come when she can, " he said softly. "She'll find her way home." *If she can,* he thought.

Chapter Twenty-Four

Always do right. This will gratify some people and astonish the rest.

—Mark Twain

Aloha explored the Little St. Simons compound with her new friend Steve Mulligan. The sun warmed her face, and she relished the rich mixture of aromas that filled the air: horses, marsh animals, birds, armadillos, and other creatures big and small.

"Look at this mess, Aloha. When do you think we'll get this all cleaned up?" he asked her, crossing his arms and looking down at her, as if waiting for an answer.

Along with the sun came the humidity. Walking away from the stables, Steve wiped his brow and continued.

"Thank God the horses are safe," he said. "Their stable proved to be as sturdy as we thought. The owners will be pleased to know that even their feed survived the hurricane."

Several windows had broken and the floors of the main house and cottages were flooded, but Steve was happy to see that Little St. Simons had not suffered a great deal of damage. As they neared the river, it became obvious that the dock area hadn't been so fortunate.

Dead fish and birds were strewn all about the land and boat area. Many small boats were under water, and broken trees and limbs had almost destroyed the dock itself. The riverbank's sand and topsoil were gone. His heart sank as he took it all in.

"Now that it's over, the workers will help me put this all back together. But what about you? Your partner must be awfully worried about you, and I can't even phone her until the lines are back up." He rubbed her face just behind the eyes, a gesture she obviously enjoyed.

After sharing a tender grilled steak, they relaxed together on the sofa. Aloha felt safe and secure but was anxious to go home.

Now that she was recovering from her wound and the traumatic ordeal of the storm, she stood up often to walk over to the screen door and whine. As night fell, her whimpering grew more persistent.

Steve knew there was nothing else he could do for her. He couldn't let her outside by herself, afraid that she might jump back into the Hampton River and try to swim home.

The telephone number on her tag indicated that she lived on St. Simons Island with a blind woman named Kimberly Louise Walker, so he knew that once the landlines were back up he could return her to her partner. Yet he understood her uneasiness, and tried to reason with her.

"Listen to me, Aloha. I promise you I'll get you home. But for now, all I can do is feed you well and keep your wound clean."

Steve added, "I lost my own best buddy last year. He was fourteen years old: a Golden Retriever. You remind me of Tanner, but you're not as rambunctious. Or, maybe you are under normal circumstances; when you haven't just survived a hurricane." Smiling, he lay down next to Aloha and rubbed her head.

"When they train you to become a guide dog, do they take away your dog character altogether, or just modify it to match your partner's? I've always wondered about that. I'm going to ask your teammate when I meet her," he mused, scratching her tummy as she rolled on her back.

Aloha looked into his smiling eyes, blinking slightly and rubbing her face against his hand.

Steve picked up his mobile phone and once again dialed the number on her tag. There was no response. The line rang once and then went silent, so he knew it was not connecting. He re-dialed it on the phone in the kitchen, but that line was completely dead. He was surprised to feel so relieved; now she would stay another night.

With a deep sigh he announced to Aloha that it was time

for bed. She followed him down the hall to the bedroom and hopped up on his bed.

Before he fell asleep, Steve thought about how soon he'd have to give Aloha back to the person who needed her. He rarely borrowed anything, but felt grateful that Aloha had been "on loan" to him briefly.

Chapter Twenty-Five

Integrity has no need of rules.
—Albert Camus

The shrill ringing of the telephone startled them.

"Shall I answer it, dear?" asked David. "Who could it be?"

"No, I'll get it," insisted Kimberly Louise, crossing the room to pick up the phone from the dresser.

"Hello?"

"Hello, is this Miss Walker?" asked a voice she didn't recognize.

"Yes, this is she," she answered with a tremulous voice, her face clouding over.

"Ma'am, I have your dog Aloha!"

Kimberly Louise sank to her knees on the bedroom floor, eyes swimming with tears. "Please let me talk to her," she asked in a strangely quiet voice.

"Sure, go ahead," prompted Steve. "She's right here by the phone."

Diego and David watched fascinated as her face softened and she began speaking.

"Aloha baby, can you hear me? Talk to me, Aloha," she commanded gently, her voice barely above a whisper.

"ARRF! WOOF! WOOF!" The barks were followed by a long desolate whine.

"Oh, thank you Lord! She's alive!" Her words were barely audible, muffled by her sobs. Turning in the direction of her friends, she nodded up and down. Diego jumped up, his eyes blazing with excitement as he ran over to Kimberly Louise.

David stood up and reached smoothly across her to remove the phone from her outstretched hand.

"Hello? Who is this please?" he asked.

"Hi, I'm Steve Mulligan, manager of the Lodge at Little St. Simons Island. Your dog was washed up on our shore, and has been here with me for several days. This is the first chance I've had to reach you since the storm," he explained.

"Is she all right?" demanded David, his eyes settling on Kimberly Louise as she wept with relief.

"Yes, she is. She came to me with a leg wound, but I've got that under control. She's sitting here next to me with cocked ears, searching for the voice of her partner. I understand that is Kimberly Louise Walker. Could you put her back on, please?"

David asked Kimberly Louise if she wanted to speak to him again. She nodded.

"Yes, I'm back," she gulped, wiping away the stream of tears coursing down her face. "Please tell me that Aloha is well."

"Ma'am, you don't need to worry about Aloha. She's fine, and I'll get her back to you just as soon as I can patch up a boat and get us over there. I have your address and you're not far from here." After repeating her address, he paused. "You sure have a sweet loving dog, Miss Walker. I'm going to miss her."

Diego couldn't contain his impatience any longer. "David, umm, Mr. Wells, can somebody tell me what's happening? Is Aloha okay?"

David put his arm around Diego's shoulders. "It certainly appears that way, son. And please call me David. Mr. Wells is much too formal."

David looked over at Kimberly Louise. "I'm sure Kimberly Louise will tell us everything once she gets off the phone."

She handed the phone back to David. Turning to Diego, she beamed. "God has answered our prayers. Aloha is well and will be home sometime this afternoon." Reaching for more tissue, she dabbed at her eyes and nose.

"Diego, now that the phone works, you need to phone home right away. I can only imagine how frustrated and worried your parents must be."

Diego picked up the phone and dialed his house. He was surprised that his father answered on the first ring.

"Papá, we're fine!" he whooped into the receiver. "We've been through a huge hurricane, but we made it, and Aloha was lost but now . . ."

Diego's father interrupted him. "Slow down, *hijo*. Is everyone okay?" he asked, confused at the mention of Aloha.

"Yes, Papá, we're fine but Aloha got lost and she's just been found. She's with some man on another barrier island because she got away from me during the storm, but he called us and said he'll bring her back when he can. Oh, Papá, it's been so hard but we're all in this together, and later I'll tell you about Miss Kimberly Louise's rattlesnake bite and how I removed the venom," he added, taking in a deep breath.

Kimberly Louise, now composed, asked Diego to pass her the phone.

"Hello, Ernesto," she began. "I want you to know that your son is a hero. He saved my life. Without him, who knows where I'd be? And our sweet Aloha will be returned to us shortly, so we're all thanking God for these miracles."

She paused. "Could you please put Maria Teresa on the phone? Diego needs to hear her comforting voice. He's had a couple of very tough days. Oh, and I want to thank you so much for sending him to me and letting me get to know him," she concluded, a smile lighting up her tired face.

Diego talked with his mother, telling her all about the last few days. When he had finished, he turned to his friends with a weary sigh.

"I can't believe that Aloha made it. Mom told me to call Jeremy, who's been really worried since he couldn't reach me on my phone. Would that be all right, since my cell phone still doesn't work?" he asked Kimberly Louise.

"Of course, Diego. But first let David make the call he's been trying to make all afternoon. He wants to ask his doctor a few questions about my snake bite, and then the phone will be yours," she murmured, rubbing David's shoulders as he rested his head in his hands.

After speaking to the doctor, David seemed greatly relieved. "He said it sounded like you did everything right, Diego, and told me to congratulate you for your excellent work!"

Turning to Kimberly Louise, he added, "Dear, he wants to give you a tetanus shot and some antibiotics. He says he will try to come by this afternoon to check on you."

Kimberly Louise grinned at Diego. "You're my hero, Diego!" she praised. "I haven't felt much pain all day, and when I touch my leg the swelling is almost gone. Tell me what color my leg is today."

Diego glanced down and saw that most of the bruising had faded.

"It's almost back to normal now," he said.

"Then let's make our phone calls and have lunch," she suggested. "Who knows how long the phones will work. I want to phone my kids and grandbabies, but you go first, while David and I get some lunch together."

David and Kimberly Louise set out crackers and cheese, carrot sticks and sliced apples while Diego enthusiastically explained the events of the past few days to his best friend in Oregon.

Kimberly Louise moved closer to David's side as they worked together in the kitchen.

"No matter how much damage we find in our homes, David, I feel so grateful to know that Aloha is safe," murmured Kimberly Louise, linking her arm through his. "You and I and Diego are safe, Mimi is somewhere far away, and I know we're all going to make it, " she said.

Reaching up to his cheek, she kissed him softly. "Thank you for coming here to be with me during this ordeal."

"Thank you for opening a door to let me come into your life," he answered, lifting her face towards his and touching his lips to hers.

From the next room, they heard the delightful sound of Diego's laughter as he shared the exciting hurricane adventures with Jeremy.

Chapter Twenty-Six

*And ye shall know the truth, and the truth
shall set you free.*

—John 8:32

Aloha let out a yelp of joy as she bounded through the door, propelled herself through the water-filled foyer and up the soggy stairs, and headed straight for Kimberly Louise, standing in the hall. Dancing wildly around her partner, she hurtled into the air and ran around in circles, giddy with delight.

"My goodness, Aloha," laughed Kimberly Louise. "What a greeting!" she exclaimed as she stooped down to embrace her ecstatic wet friend.

Steve stood in the doorway, overwhelmed by this heart-warming show of devotion. Diego watched quietly from the bed, wishing he could participate in the emotional welcome.

David finally broke the spell.

"Sir, didn't you tell me she was injured?" he asked Steve.

"You'd never know it by that greeting, would you?" Steve chuckled. "She didn't even limp as she flew across the room, but I can assure you she's been limping ever since the morning she walked up my front steps."

As soon as Kimberly Louise touched her fingers lightly to Aloha's wet nose, the dog settled down at her side and stood as solid as a statue, her shoulder touching Kimberly Louise's leg with all four paws supporting her. Her face was turned straight upwards and she was looking at her mistress upside-down. Kimberly Louise's murmured encouragement had shifted Aloha back into the highly trained caregiver she was bred to be.

Diego marveled at Aloha's faithfulness. He had learned during his puppy raising training that a deep seated canine instinct makes a dog recognize and honor her companion as absolute master and lord. Still, he couldn't help feeling a lump in his throat as Aloha gave Kimberly Louise her undivided attention.

"Aloha, go say hello to Diego and David," she commanded softly, speaking directly into her partner's ear and stroking her head.

Aloha pricked her ears forward and rushed to Diego's side, quivering from head to tail and standing up on her hind legs. She placed her paws on his shoulder and touched her nose to his. Diego hugged her tightly, burying his face in her damp fur. Aloha licked the side of his face and neck. When Diego finally released her, he noticed she was still gazing intently at him.

"Good girl, *muchachita*," whispered Diego. "I know you've forgiven me for losing you." He kissed her nose. "Now go see David."

Aloha again obeyed. She trotted over to David and rubbed her face in his hands, wagging her tail as fast as she could. Then she lay down, rolled over and put her feet in the air, begging him to scratch her tummy.

They laughed with happiness; then they turned their attention to Steve, still standing in the doorway downstairs.

"Mr. Mulligan," began Kimberly Louise. "We haven't even thanked you for what you've done for us. Please come upstairs and sit with us where it's drier."

"You don't need to thank me for anything, Ma'am. I did what anyone would do. And I enjoyed every moment with Aloha," he smiled gravely. "But I've got to head back to Little St. Simons Island and start cleaning up the mess. Will you have some help getting your house back in shape?" he wondered, waving his hand to indicate the debris and damage throughout the house.

"Yes, we'll help her," answered David and Diego.

David explained. "We'll take Kimberly Louise and Aloha to higher ground; then we'll worry about the house and her belongings once the water subsides." He paused, and smiled.

"I also want to thank you for your compassion and your kindness in bringing Aloha home so quickly. Please leave us your phone number so we can keep in touch."

Kimberly Louise added, "And come by anytime to visit us and Aloha. Maybe we can come over to visit you too. I've always wanted to go over there and see your island for myself."

Diego smiled, loving how Kimberly Louise often used the word "see," knowing that even though she did not have use of her eyes she "saw" as well as anyone. He knew that Kimberly Louise felt and experienced life through her other senses, probably treasuring her blessings just like anyone else. She and Aloha had come so far in such a short time.

"Goodbye, Mr. Mulligan," added Diego. "Thanks again for bringing Aloha back home safely."

Aloha, hearing her name, cocked her ears and lifted her head from her paws, thumping her tail from side to side.

When Steve walked up the steps to say goodbye, Aloha rose to meet him and licked his hands and face. She said goodbye to him three times, offering both paws, one after another, then stretching to place them on his shoulders.

"You're welcome, Aloha," Steve muttered, his voice cracking. "Come back to see me soon."

Diego closed his tired eyes and smiled, happy he had captured that tender moment with his camera.

Chapter Twenty-Seven

What is a friend? A single soul in two bodies.

—Aristotle

Diego's last few days in Georgia flew by as they worked on repairing Kimberly Louise's house. David urged her to move from the damaged home into Mimi's house, but she insisted on staying with them to help clean up. Mimi returned to St. Simons Island and spent a large part of every day working with them. Mimi's house wasn't as close to the water and had sustained much less damage.

Two days before Diego was scheduled to fly out of Jacksonville, Kimberly Louise announced that she had a surprise for him.

"Pack your suitcase tonight, Diego, because tomorrow we're going on an unexpected trip," she announced with her broad grin. "Mimi and David will join us, and from there we'll take you to the airport on Sunday."

"Where are we going?" asked Diego. "Does everyone else know except me?"

"Now, Diego, if I tell you it won't be a surprise, will it? Don't take that pleasure away from us after all our planning," she chided.

Diego returned to his room and slowly packed his clothes and treasures from St. Simons Island: small gifts from Kimberly Louise, the kite Mimi had bought him, the books about the area, a photograph of Courtney and him in the Okefenokee Swamp, his photos and the newspaper articles about the hurricane. In his bathroom he rinsed and dried the colorful seashells he had discovered after the storm, scattered over the dunes.

Aloha walked in, sniffing the air.

"Oh, girl, can you smell the creatures that lived in these shells?" he grinned. Kneeling down to pet her, he looked at her with a melancholy expression.

"Now I have to let you go all over again," he whispered, hugging her. "But at least I know you'll never forget me either."

Standing up, Diego cleared his throat. "And we'll be together tomorrow on this surprise trip—the one neither one of us knows anything about." He laughed, "It's like we're the blind ones and they're leading us," he joked.

The phone rang. It was Courtney, asking if she could come over to say goodbye.

Diego met her at the door and suggested they sit on the

porch. Courtney bashfully handed him a small bag stuffed with tissue paper.

"Open it," she encouraged.

Diego shrugged and smiled self-consciously. "What is it?" he wondered.

Pulling off the tissue he lifted out a framed picture of Aloha and him, taken the day they visited Jekyll Island. His arms were wrapped around her neck and she was licking his face.

"That's so cool! And I don't have a picture like this!" he exclaimed, delighted. Turning to face her, Diego added, "Courtney, thank you."

She grinned broadly and told him she would email him soon. After she left, Diego returned to finish his packing.

The next day, as they were driving across the bridge that marked the Florida border, Mimi turned around in her seat and covered Diego's eyes with a handkerchief.

"Just a little further, Diego. It will be more fun for you this way," smiled Kimberly Louise.

Finally, the car slowed down and turned sharply before coming to a stop. Aloha, who had been sitting on Diego's feet for the past half hour, climbed onto his lap, concerned about the handkerchief covering his eyes.

"Go ahead and take off the blindfold now," Mimi told him.

Diego slid the blindfold over his eyes and nose and read: *Welcome to the Jacksonville Zoo and Gardens.*

"Did I win the bet?" he asked, suddenly remembering the bet they made on the amount of rainfall during the hurricane.

"Actually no, you lost," laughed Kimberly Louise. "But you've already paid up by helping me clean the house.

"Who won?" asked Diego and David simultaneously.

"Why, I did! Over fifty inches of water fell during Hurricane Karin, and I bet fifty or more."

"Yes you did dear, so it looks like I'm inviting y'all to the zoo," declared David.

"O.K., but I won that it was a Category Four hurricane, right?" countered Diego.

"Hmm, I don't remember betting on that, do you David? Perhaps that happened during my delirium right after the snakebite," teased Kimberly Louise.

They enjoyed a happy, stimulating day walking through the zoo and botanical gardens. With elephants, giraffes and white rhinos, it was like a walking safari. There were over one thousand rare exotic animals and plant varieties.

During the hottest part of the afternoon, Diego ran through the water park to cool off while the others sat in the shade. Then Diego asked the attendant if he could take Aloha on leash to the nearest water shower.

"Of course you can," was the quick reply.

Aloha romped happily through the fountain.

"*Muchachita*, I thought you might be scared of water after

your river crossing to Little St. Simons Island," said Diego, running his hands over Aloha's wet fur. "But I was wrong."

"My favorite part is the Emerald Forest Aviary," exclaimed Mimi, sitting on the sidelines with David and Kimberly Louise. "It's so awesome to watch the yellow-billed storks, flamingos and turacos!"

Kimberly Louise's friends took turns describing the African animals and plants to her, and she enjoyed every moment of her last day with Diego.

That evening they dined at one of their favorite Italian restaurants. As usual, Aloha received a great deal of attention. Diego remembered how he had handled it when he was her puppy raiser, and admired how well Kimberly Louise was dealing with so many questions. There were moments when he saw Aloha looking up at him, and he wondered if she were sharing his memories.

They stayed in a motel minutes away from the airport. Mimi, Aloha and Kimberly Louise said goodnight and went to their room. Diego and David sat on the patio, enjoying the shimmering full moon.

"Kimberly Louise is going to miss you, son. This has been the happiest I've seen her since her accident. With you and Aloha by her side, she's experienced things this past month that she'd only imagined."

"Really? *I've* also experienced things I never thought I'd do, including Hurricane Karin!" chuckled Diego. Frowning, he added, "But saying goodbye will be hard, since I've really become her friend, and yours too." Diego looked away, thinking of Aloha.

"And that's the wonderful part of friendship," offered David. "Now we'll look forward to our next time together. In fact, when you return I'll take all of us over to stay at the Lodge at Little St. Simons Island for a weekend! They say it's incredible and we already know the manager. What do you say?"

Diego smiled and said he would look forward to that.

"David, remember a few days ago when I told you that I might get another puppy to raise for Guide Dogs?"

"Yes, I remember," said David.

"I'm having a real hard time making a decision. It just seems like so much work for just a few months of having the dog."

David remained silent for a long moment. "Diego, you don't have to decide now, or even in a few months," he offered, sympathizing with Diego's dilemma.

Diego nodded and looked up at him. A new plan was formulating in his mind.

"David, if you and Miss Kimberly Louise get married, would you like to honeymoon in Oregon? I have friends on the coast who would let you use their beach house, and then I could see you both and Aloha too!"

"What a jolly good idea," beamed David. "I'll mention it

to her the minute your plane taxis out, and I'll email you her answer even before it touches down in Portland."

Diego reached over to embrace him. He decided that this long distance friendship was going to be all right after all.

Chapter Twenty-Eight

The journey is the reward.
—Chinese Proverb

Diego, Jeremy and Clara sat in the den poring over Diego's photos of Hurricane Karin.

"Didn't you take any the day Aloha got lost?" asked Clara.

"Of course not, Clara. It was hard enough holding her leash in those winds. And we weren't just out for an afternoon stroll, you know."

"But your friend Courtney could have taken pictures while you walked Aloha. Then you'd have a complete photo record of the hurricane, from beginning to end," she insisted.

Diego shook his head in annoyance. Although his sister was now almost twelve, she was starting to remind him of seven-year-old Tyler, and he told her so.

Jeremy intervened. "Hey, Clara, maybe you can use these

pictures to do a report on hurricanes next year in school. You'd almost have a firsthand account."

Clara smiled. "Good idea, Jeremy. And I can use part of Diego's term paper for the scientific details, can't I Diego?"

"Sure, Clara," said Diego, distracted. Studying the vivid images of the hurricane, it seemed like it had happened months ago, not just two weeks. He shuddered, reliving those long agonizing days without Aloha, the torment he endured believing she might have died, and the horror of the snakebite.

"Diego, are you still with us?" asked Clara impatiently. "Jeremy just asked you who this guy with the beard is who's hugging Aloha."

"Oh, that's Steve, the man who brought her back from Little St. Simons Island. I took that picture when he brought Aloha back. She was telling him goodbye," he smiled.

In the three days since his return, he had been so busy he hadn't really missed Aloha. But now, looking at pictures of her, the wound was reopened.

"Kimberly Louise looks so happy with David," commented Maria Teresa as she entered the room and leaned over the coffee table to look at the photos. "Are they already engaged?"

"No, Mamá, not that I know of. But I hope they will be soon, because I've already invited them out here to spend their honeymoon."

Maria Teresa raised an eyebrow. "Here, in our house?"

Diego chuckled. "Not exactly. I kinda suggested the Bakers' beach house in Manzanita. I thought that would be a great place for Aloha to run and . . ."

"And for you to join them, perhaps?" chuckled his mother.

"Diego, you can't join couples on their honeymoon!" scolded Clara, hands on her hips.

Diego reddened. "You really do remind me of Tyler," he retorted, turning to face her. "Always sticking your nose into other people's conversations."

Clara threw him a wounded look as she huffed out of the room.

"Well now, I see it's a lovely day outside," said Maria Teresa, her voice breaking through the uncomfortable silence. "You boys might like to take a bike ride over to the lake. And while you're there, could you please pick up a few items from the store?"

"Sure, Mrs. Escobár. Come on, Diego. Let's put some air in the tires first."

Diego suddenly remembered David's promise to email him about his marriage proposal to Miss Kimberly Louise. Hadn't he told him he was going to ask her the same day he left?

"Go ahead, Jeremy. I'll meet you at your house in ten minutes. I just want to check my email."

There were two new emails: one from Kimberly Louise

161

and one from Courtney. Diego read enthusiastically that Aloha continued to wander into his bedroom and jump up on his bed. Kimberly Louise also wrote that David had taken Mimi and her to lunch after his plane left, but she didn't say anything more about David.

Courtney sent Diego a long email describing her school activities, teachers and classes. Schools in Georgia began their school curriculum in August. Diego's heart skipped a beat when she told him she "missed" him and hoped he would come back soon. Then she wrote: *What have you decided to do about getting another puppy?* He liked reading her email but wasn't sure how her inquisitive words made him feel. He decided he would answer her later.

The one email he was waiting for wasn't there. David had told him he'd write or phone as soon as the plane touched down in Portland, three days ago. Had he already forgotten him?

Jeremy's dog Alma ran alongside the boys as they biked through the forest and down to the lake. She was Aloha's sister and had not made it through formal guide dog training, so Jeremy got to keep her. Most of the time that didn't bother Diego, but today it did. Diego felt a pang of resentment and annoyance. Alma looked so much like Aloha, and watching her run at Jeremy's side made him sad.

After the ride, Diego made excuses to go home. Clara, spying from the window, rushed out the door to meet him.

"Hey, Diego, you just got a phone call from Kimberly Louise and Mr. Wells. They want you to phone them right away!" she chattered.

"Do you know what it's about?" asked Diego.

Her eyes twinkled. "Nope, they wouldn't tell me, but they were both giggling like little kids."

Diego went into his bedroom, shut the door and dialed Kimberly Louise's number. As the call went through, he closed his eyes and hoped for good news.

"Hello Diego! How are you, dear?" asked Kimberly Louise. "Do you have any idea how much we all miss you? Don't we, darling?" She must have been talking to David.

"Yes, Aloha and I miss you too," answered David, in his rich mellow voice. "Here, talk to her," he encouraged.

"Aloha, *mi querida muchacha* (my dear little girl), can you hear me?" said Diego, his voice cracking with emotion.

"WOOF! WOOF!" Aloha responded instantly, recognizing his voice.

"Oh, girl, I miss you too, but just be patient and we'll see each other soon, *si Diós quiere* (God willing)."

Kimberly Louise removed the receiver from David's hand. "Diego, David and I have some news for you, and we want you to know that after our kids and Mimi, you are the next to be told!"

Diego held his breath. Finally exhaling, he mumbled, "What news?"

"Oh sweetie, David's asked me to marry him! Isn't that wonderful?"

"And what did you say, Miss Kimberly Louise?" Again he held his breath, afraid he'd miss her answer.

"Well, I told him I'd be honored to be his wife," she burbled. "I said I wanted you to know right away, because you are so much a part of Aloha. And then he told me that he had already promised to tell you as soon as I accepted. Isn't that amazing?"

Diego sat composed for just a moment to take it all in. At last he said, "I'm so happy for you, Miss Kimberly Louise. It's perfect! You two are great together! Where and when will you get married?"

David took the phone from his fiancée's hand. "Diego, we will marry over the Christmas holidays, when our families can join us. It will be a small wedding, and then we'll get on a plane and fly out to Oregon, where we'll celebrate with you. Remember, you promised to get us that beach house on the Oregon coast, and we'd be thrilled if you and your family could join us there for the New Year's celebration."

Diego couldn't believe this awesome news. In just four months, he and Aloha would be together again! His new friends were marrying, and they would all be coming to Oregon to celebrate the New Year!

"Diego, are you there?" asked David.

"Yes, David. It's just such great news!" answered Diego

softly. "I'm feeling overwhelmed, like the day Miss Kimberly Louise told me about the fullness of hope."

David was quiet a long moment. "And did she tell you about the redwoods?"

"Yes. How they hold each other up in strength. That's what you've done with me," he acknowledged.

"And that's what your gift of love has done for us—for all of us," said David.

Diego no longer fought the welling tears. "Thank you, David. Tell Miss Kimberly Louise I'm beginning to understand what she meant when she said '*to live is to change.*' That's made me more hopeful about life."

David listened, respecting his feelings.

"And David, I have something to tell you, too. Remember what we talked about that day during the hurricane? About getting another guide puppy?"

"Yes, Diego. I remember. Have you come to a decision?"

"Yes. Could you please put Miss Kimberly Louise on another extension?" asked Diego. He waited nervously until he knew they were both listening.

"Today, right before I called you, I felt it was finally time for me to raise another guide puppy," began Diego tentatively. "I haven't even told my family yet, or asked them, I should say," he tittered. "But I know they'll be happy with my decision. I have to move on with my life, and part of that is really releasing Aloha to you."

Finally, Kimberly Louise spoke.

"Congratulations, Diego! That's wonderful news! We'll love sharing Aloha with you and getting to know your new puppy. Just think of all the fun we'll have in December. I hope you have her by then!"

"Me too. Could you please tell Aloha she opened up an important place in my heart and will always live there?"

David heard the raw emotion in Diego's voice.

"You tell her, son. She's standing at my side, ears pricked, wanting to hear it from you."

Resources

Printed Word

The following books were invaluable to my research. They may also be helpful to adults and young readers.

A Dog's Life, Peter Mayle, Alfred A. Knoff. 1995

Book of Storms, Eric Sloane, Duell, Sloan & Pearce. 1956

Breach of Faith: Hurricane Katrina And The Near Death Of A Great American City, Jed Horne, Random House. 2006

Carolina Hurricane, Marian Rumsey, William Morrow & Co. Inc. 1979

Follow My Leader, James B. Garfield, Puffin Books. 1957

Hurricane, Jonathan London, Lothrop, Lee & Shepard Books. 1998

Hurricane, Karen Harper, MIRA Books. 2006

Killer Cane: The Deadly Hurricane of 1928, Robert Mykle, Cooper Square Press. 2002

Lad: A Dog, Albert Payson Terhune, G.K. Hall & Co. 1962

Old Yeller, Fred Gipson, Harper Collins Publishers Inc. 1956

Partners In Independence: A Success Story of Dogs and the Disabled, Ed & Toni Eames, Barkleigh Productions. 1997

Second Wind, Dick Francis, G.P. Putnam's Sons. 1999

Sight Hound, Pam Houston, W.W. Norton & Co. 2005

Snakes of the Southeast, Whit Gibbons and Mike Dorcas, University of Georgia Press. 2005

Sounder, William Armstrong, Harper & Row. 1969

Stay! Keeper's Story, Lois Lowry, Houghton Mifflin Co. 1997

Storm at the Jetty, Leonard Everett Fisher, The Viking Press. 1981

Storm of the Century: The Labor Day Hurricane of 1985, Willie Drye, National Geographic Society. 2002

The Coming Storm, Bob Reiss, Hyperion. 2001

The Fireside Book of Dog Stories: Gulliver The Great, Walter A. Dyer, Simon & Schuster, Inc. 1943

The Gospel According To Brodie: Lessons From A Blind Labrador, Jennifer Rees Larcombe, Marshall Pickering. 1995

The Magic School Bus Inside A Hurricane, Joanna Cole, Scholastic. 1995

The Mystery of the Double Double Cross, Mary Blount Christian, Albert Whitman & Co. 1982

Weather Explained, Derek Elsom, Henry Holt & Company, Inc. 1997

Articles

Biography "Louis Braille: A Touch of Genius" from National Braille Press, Wikipedia Encyclopedia. 2007

The Bag, DeAnna Quietwater Noriega, Colorado Springs, Co. 2006

Trusting Tanner, Rebecca Kragnes, Petwarmers Website. 2006

Interviews

Dana Gantt, Sight-impaired partner of Quint, Atlanta, GA

Dr. Jon Traer, MD, Darien, GA

Michael Hingson, National Public Affairs Director-Guide Dogs for the Blind, San Rafael, CA

Guide Dog Schools

CALIFORNIA

Eye Dog Foundation
512 N. Larchmont Blvd.
Los Angeles, CA 90004
(213) 468-1012
www.eyedogfoundation.org

Guide Dogs for the Blind
350 Los Ranchitos Road, San Rafael, CA 94903
32901 S.E. Kelso Road, Boring, OR 97009
(800) 295-4050
www.guidedogs.com

Guide Dogs of the Desert
PO Box 1692
Palm Springs, CA 92263
(619) 329-6257
www.guidedogsofthedesert.org

Guide Dogs of America
13445 Glenoaks Boulevard
Sylmar, CA 91342
(818) 362-5834
www.guidedogsofamerica.org

CONNECTICUT

Fidelco Guide Dog Foundation
P.O. Box 142
Bloomfield, CT 06002
(203) 243-5200
www.fidelco.org

FLORIDA

Southeastern Guide Dogs
4210 77th Street East
Palmetto, FL 34221
(813) 729-5665
www.southeasternguidedogs.org

HAWAII

Eye of the Pacific Guide Dogs & Mobility Services, Inc.
747 Amana Street, #407
Honolulu, HI 96814
(808) 941-1088
www.eyeofthepacific.org

KANSAS

Kansas Specialty Dog Service
123 West 7th, Box 216
Washington, KS 66968
(913) 325-2256
www.gdui.org

MICHIGAN

Leader Dogs for the Blind
1039 South Rochester Rd.
Rochester, MI 48307
(313) 651-9011
www.leaderdog.org

NEW JERSEY

The Seeing Eye, Inc.
Washington Valley Road
Morristown, NJ 07960
(201) 539-4425
www.seeingeye.org

NEW YORK

Guide Dog Foundation for the Blind
371 East Jericho Turnpike
Smithtown, NY 11787
(800) 548-4337
www.guidedog.org

Guiding Eyes for the Blind
611 Granite Springs Road
Yorktown Heights, NY 10598
(914) 245-4024
www.guidingeyes.org

Freedom Guide Dogs for the Blind
1210 Hardscrabble Road
Cassville, NY 13318
(315) 822-5132
www.freedomguidedogs.org

OHIO

Pilot Dogs, Inc.
625 West Town Street
Columbus, OH 43215-4496
(614) 221-6367
www.healthfinder.gov/org

TEXAS

Guide Dogs of Texas, Inc.
11825 West Avenue Suite 104
San Antonio, TX 78216
(210) 366-4082
www.guidedogsoftexas.org

CANADA

Canadian Guide Dogs for the Blind
National Office and Training Centre
P.O. Box 280
4120 Rideau Valley Drive N.
Manotick, Ontario
K4M 1A3
(613) 692-7777
www.guidedogs.ca

Lions Foundation of Canada Canine Vision Canada
P.O. Box 907
Oakville, Ontario
L6J 5E8
(800) 768-3030
www.dogguides.com

Western Guide and Assistance Dog Society
14550 – 116 Avenue
Edmonton, Alberta T5M 3E9
Phone: (780) 944-8011
www.guidedog.ca

IRELAND

Irish Guide dogs for the BlindNational Headquarters
and Training Centre
Model Farm Road
Cork
telephone: 353 21 4878200
www.guidedogs.ie

International Federation of Guide Dog Schools for the Blind
www.ifgdsb.org.uk

About the Artist

Ian Kaszans is the owner of Kazuma Gallery in historic downtown Brunswick, Georgia. He is a 2006 graduate of Savannah College of Art & Design with a Master's Degree in Illustration. His illustrations have won awards throughout the Coastal Empire. Ian is active in several organizations and has done illustrative work for Hospice of the Golden Isles, Historic Brunswick Business Association, Signature Squares of Brunswick, and Honey Creek. In addition to the local illustrations, Ian has also designed graphics and logos for companies around the US. To learn more about Ian Kaszans, visit www.iankaszans.com.

About The Author

Pamela Bauer Mueller resides on Jekyll Island, Georgia with her husband Michael and their two cats, Jasper and Sukey Spice. She was raised in Oregon and graduated from Lewis and Clark College in Portland, Oregon. She worked as a flight attendant for Pan American Airlines before marrying and moving to Mexico City, where she lived for eighteen years, teaching English and Spanish, modeling and acting in U.S. and Mexican television and films.

After returning to the United States, Pamela worked for twelve years as a U.S. Customs Inspector, serving in San Diego and in Vancouver, B. C. Canada. Pamela took an early retirement to follow her husband Michael, who received an instructor position at the Federal Law Enforcement Training Center in Brunswick, Georgia.

Pamela's children's books include *The Kiska Trilogy* and *Hello, Goodbye, I Love You.* She wrote *Neptune's Honor* and *An Angry Drum Echoed* as Y/A historical novels, based on the lives of actual residents of Georgia: Neptune Small, a noble antebellum-era slave who shared a special bond with his master's son, and Mary Musgrove, a Creek/English-woman who played a significant role in Georgia's colonial history.